THE WORKS OF ANATOLE FRANCE IN AN ENGLISH TRANSLATION EDITED BY JAMES LEWIS MAY AND BERNARD MIALL

THE SEVEN WIVES OF BLUEBEARD

THE SEVEN WIVES OF BLUEBEARD & OTHER MARVELLOUS TALES

BY ANATOLE FRANCE

A TRANSLATION BY
D. B. STEWART

LONDON: JOHN LANE, THE BODLEY HEAD
NEW YORK: JOHN LANE COMPANY MCMXX

The Mayflower Press, Plymouth, England. William Brendon & Son, Ltd.

CONTENTS

CONTENTS

THE SEVEN WIVES OF BLUEBEARD

THE SEVEN WIVES OF BLUEBEARD

CHAPTER I

THE strangest, the most varied, the most erroneous opinions have been expressed with regard to the famous individual commonly known as Bluebeard. None, perhaps, was less tenable than that which made of this gentleman a personification of the Sun. For this is what a certain school of comparative mythology set itself to do, some forty years ago. It informed the world that the seven wives of Bluebeard were the Dawns, and that his two brothers-in-law were the morning and the evening Twilight, identifying them with the Dioscuri, who delivered Helena when she was rapt away by Theseus. We must remind those readers who may feel tempted to believe this that in 1817 a learned librarian of Agen, Jean-Baptiste Pérés, demonstrated, in a highly plausible manner, that Napoleon had never existed, and that the story of this supposed great captain was nothing but a solar myth. Despite the most ingenious diversions of the wits, we cannot possibly doubt that Bluebeard and Napoleon did both actually exist.

An hypothesis no better founded is that which consists in identifying Bluebeard with the Marshal de Rais, who was strangled by the arm of the Law above the bridges of Nantes on 26th of October, 1440. Without inquiring, with M. Salomon Reinach, whether the Marshal committed the crimes for which he was condemned, or whether his wealth, coveted by a greedy prince, did not in some degree contribute to his undoing, there is nothing in his life that resembles what we find in Bluebeard's; this alone is enough to prevent our confusing them or merging the two individuals into one.

Charles Perrault, who, about 1660, had the merit of composing the first biography of this *seigneur*, justly remarkable for having married seven wives, made him an accomplished villain, and the most perfect model of cruelty that ever trod the earth. But it is permissible to doubt, if not his sincerity, at least the correctness of his information. He may, perhaps, have been prejudiced against his hero. He would not have been the first example of a poet or historian who liked to darken the colours of his pictures. If we have what seems a flattering portrait of Titus, it would seem, on the other hand, that Tacitus has painted Tiberius much blacker than the reality. Macbeth, whom legend and Shakespeare accuse of crimes, was in reality a just and a wise king. He never treacherously murdered the old king, Duncan. Duncan, while yet young, was defeated in a great battle, and was found dead on the morrow at a spot called the Armourer's Shop. He had slain several of the kinsfolk of Gruchno, the wife of Macbeth. The latter made Scotland prosperous; he encouraged trade, and was regarded as the defender of the middle classes, the true King of the townsmen. The nobles of the clans never forgave him for defeating Duncan, nor for protecting the artisans. They destroyed him, and dishonoured his memory. Once he was dead the good King Macbeth was known only by the statements of his enemies. The genius of Shakespeare imposed these lies upon the human consciousness. I had long suspected that Bluebeard was the victim of a similar fatality. All the circumstances of his life, as I found them related, were far from satisfying my mind, and from gratifying that craving for logic and lucidity by which I am incessantly consumed. On reflection, I perceived that they involved insurmountable difficulties. There was so great a desire to make me believe in the man's cruelty that it could not fail to make me doubt it.

These presentiments did not mislead me. My intuitions, which had their origin in a certain knowledge of human nature, were soon to be changed into certainty, based upon irrefutable proofs.

In the house of a stone-cutter in St. Jean-des-Bois, I found several papers relating to Bluebeard; amongst others his defence, and an anonymous complaint against his murderers, which was not proceeded with, for what reasons I know not. These papers confirmed me in the belief that he was good and unfortunate, and that his memory has been overwhelmed by unworthy slanders. From that time forth, I regarded it as my duty to write his true history, without permitting myself any illusion as to the success of such an undertaking. I am well aware that this attempt at rehabilitation is destined to fall into silence and oblivion. How can the cold, naked Truth fight against the glittering enchantments of Falsehood?

CHAPTER II

SOMEWHERE about 1650 there lived on his estate, between Compiègne and Pierrefonds, a wealthy noble, by name Bernard de Montragoux, whose ancestors had held the most important posts in the kingdom. But he dwelt far from the Court, in that peaceful obscurity which then veiled all save that on which the king bestowed his glance. His castle of Guillettes abounded in valuable furniture, gold and silver ware, tapestry and embroideries, which he kept in coffers; not that he hid his treasures for fear of damaging them by use; he was, on the contrary, generous and magnificent. But in those days, in the country, the nobles willingly led a very simple life, feeding their people at their own table, and dancing on Sundays with the girls of the village.

On certain occasions, however, they gave splendid entertainments, which contrasted with the dullness of everyday life. So it was necessary that they should hold a good deal of handsome furniture and beautiful tapestries in reserve. This was the case with Monsieur de Montragoux.

His castle, built in the Gothic period, had all its rudeness. From without it looked wild and gloomy enough, with the stumps of its great towers, which had been thrown down at the time of the monarchy's troubles, in the reign of the late King Louis. Within it offered a much pleasanter prospect. The rooms were decorated in the Italian taste, as was the great gallery on the ground floor, loaded with embossed decorations in high relief, pictures and gilding.

At one end of this gallery there was a closet usually known as " the little cabinet." This is the only name by which Charles Perrault refers to it. It is as well to note that it was also called the " Cabinet of the Unfortunate Princesses," because a Florentine painter had portrayed on the walls the tragic stories of Dirce, daughter of the Sun, bound by the sons of Antiope to the horns of a bull, Niobe weeping on Mount Sipylus for her children, pierced by the divine arrows, and Procris inviting to her bosom the javelin of Cephalus. These figures had a look of life about them, and the porphyry tiles with which the floor was covered seemed dyed in the blood of these unhappy women. One of the doors of the Cabinet gave upon the moat, which had no water in it.

The stables formed a sumptuous building, situated at some distance from the castle. They contained stalls for sixty horses, and coach-houses for twelve gilded coaches. But what made Guillettes so bewitching a residence were the woods and canals surrounding it, in which one could devote oneself to the pleasures of angling and the chase.

Many of the dwellers in that country-side knew Monsieur de Montragoux only by the name of Bluebeard, for this was the only name that the common people gave him. And in truth his beard was blue, but it was blue only because it was black, and it was because it was so black that it was blue. Monsieur de Montragoux must not be imagined as having the monstrous aspect of the threefold Typhon whom one sees in Athens, laughing in his triple indigo-blue beard. We shall get much nearer the reality by comparing the *seigneur* of Guillettes to those actors or priests whose freshly shaven cheeks have a bluish gloss.

Monsieur de Montragoux did not wear a pointed beard like his grandfather at the Court of King Henry II; nor did he wear it like a fan, as did his great-grandfather who was killed at the battle of Marignan. Like Monsieur de Turenne, he had only a slight moustache, and a chin-tuft; his cheeks had a bluish look; but whatever may have been said of him, this good gentleman was by no means disfigured thereby, nor did he inspire any fear on that account. He only looked the more virile, and if it made him look a little fierce, it had not the effect of making the women dislike him. Bernard de Montragoux was a very fine man, tall, broad across the shoulders, moderately stout, and well favoured; albeit of a rustic habit, smacking of the woods rather than of drawing-rooms and assemblies. Still, it is true that he did not please the ladies as much as he should have pleased them, built as he was, and wealthy. Shyness was the reason; shyness, not his beard. Women exercised an invincible attraction for him, and at the same time inspired him with an insuperable fear. He feared them as much as he loved them. This was the origin and initial cause of all his misfortunes. Seeing a lady for the first time, he would have died rather than speak to her, and however much attracted he may have been, he stood before her in gloomy silence. His feelings revealed themselves only through his eyes, which he rolled in a terrible manner. This timidity exposed him to every kind of misfortune, and, above all, it prevented his forming a becoming connection with modest and reserved women; and betrayed him, defenceless, to the attempts of the most impudent and audacious. This was his life's misfortune.

Left an orphan from his early youth, and having rejected, owing to this sort of bashfulness and fear, which he was unable to overcome, the very advantageous and honourable alliances which had presented themselves, he married a Mademoiselle Colette Passage, who had recently settled down in that part of the country, after amassing a little money by making a bear dance through the towns and villages of the kingdom. He loved her with all his soul. And to do her justice, there was something pleasing about her, though she was what she was: a fine woman with an ample bosom, and a complexion that was still sufficiently fresh, although a little sunburnt by the open air. Great were her joy and surprise on first becoming a lady of quality. Her heart, which was not bad, was touched by the kindness of a husband in such a high position, and with such a stout, powerful body, who was to her the most obedient of servants and devoted of lovers. But after a few months she grew weary because she could no longer go to and fro on the face of the earth. In the midst of wealth, overwhelmed with love and care, she could find no greater pleasure than that of going to see the companion of her wandering life, in the cellar where he languished with a chain round his neck and a ring through his nose, and kissing him on the eyes and weeping.

Seeing her full of care, Monsieur de Montragoux himself became careworn, and this only added to his companion's melancholy. The consideration and forethought which he lavished on her turned the poor woman's head. One morning, when he awoke, Monsieur de Montragoux found Colette no longer at his side. In vain he searched for her throughout the castle.

The door of the Cabinet of the Unfortunate Princesses was open. It was through this door that she had gone to reach the open country with her bear. The sorrow of Bluebeard was painful to behold. In spite of the innumerable messengers sent forth in search of her, no news was ever received of Colette Passage.

Monsieur de Montragoux was still mourning her when he happened to dance, at the fair of Guillettes, with Jeanne de La Cloche, daughter of the Police Lieutenant of Compiègne, who inspired him with love. He asked her in marriage, and obtained her forthwith. She loved wine, and drank it to excess. So much did this taste increase that after a few months she looked like a leather bottle with a round red face atop of it. The worst of it was that this leather bottle would run mad, incessantly rolling about the reception-rooms and the staircases, crying, swearing, and hiccoughing; vomiting wine and insults at everything that got in her way. Monsieur de Montragoux was dazed with disgust and horror. But he quite suddenly recovered his courage, and set himself, with as much firmness as patience, to cure his wife of so disgusting a vice. Prayers, remonstrances, supplications, and threats: he employed every possible means. All was useless. He forbade her wine from his cellar: she got it from outside, and was more abominably drunk than ever.

To deprive her of her taste for a beverage that she loved too well, he put valerian in the bottles. She thought he was trying to poison her, sprang upon him, and drove three inches of kitchen knife into his belly. He expected to die of it, but he did not abandon his habitual kindness.

"She is more to be pitied than blamed," he said.

One day, when he had forgotten to close the door of the Cabinet of the Unfortunate Princesses, Jeanne de La Cloche entered by it, quite out of her mind, as usual, and seeing the figures on the walls in postures of affliction, ready to give up the ghost, she mistook them for living women, and fled terror-stricken into the country, screaming murder. Hearing Bluebeard calling her and running after her, she threw herself, mad with terror, into a pond, and was there drowned. It is difficult to believe, yet certain, that her husband, so compassionate was his soul, was much afflicted by her death.

Six weeks after the accident he quietly married Gigonne, the daughter of his steward, Traignel. She wore wooden shoes, and smelt of onions. She was a fine-looking girl enough, except that she squinted with one eye, and limped with one foot. As soon as she was married, this goose-girl, bitten by foolish ambition, dreamed of nothing but further greatness and splendour. She was not satisfied that her brocade dresses were rich enough, her pearl necklaces beautiful enough, her rubies big enough, her coaches sufficiently gilded, her lakes, woods, and lands sufficiently vast. Bluebeard, who had never had any leaning toward ambition, trembled at the haughty humour of his spouse. Unaware, in his straightforward simplicity, whether the mistake lay in thinking magnificently like his wife, or modestly as he himself did, he accused himself of a mediocrity of mind which was thwarting the noble desires of his consort, and, full of uncertainty, he would sometimes exhort her to taste with moderation the good things of this world, while at others he roused himself to pursue fortune along the verge of precipitous heights. He was prudent, but conjugal affection bore him beyond the reach of prudence. Gigonne thought of nothing but cutting a figure in the world, being received at Court, and becoming the King's mistress. Unable to gain her point, she pined away with vexation, contracting a jaundice, of which she died. Bluebeard, full of lamentation, built her a magnificent tomb.

This worthy *seigneur*, overwhelmed by constant domestic adversity, would not perhaps have chosen another wife: but he was himself chosen for a husband by Mademoiselle Blanche de Gibeaumex, the daughter of a cavalry officer, who had but one ear; he used to relate that he had lost the other in the King's service. She was full of intelligence, which she employed in deceiving her husband. She betrayed him with every man of quality in the neighbourhood. She was so dexterous that she deceived him in his own castle, almost under his very eyes, without his perceiving it. Poor Bluebeard assuredly suspected something, but he could not say what. Unfortunately for her, while she gave her whole mind to tricking her husband, she was not sufficiently careful in deceiving her lovers; by which I mean that she betrayed them, one for another. One day she was surprised in the Cabinet of the Unfortunate Princesses, in the company of a gentleman whom she loved, by a gentleman whom she had loved, and the latter, in a transport of jealousy, ran her through with his sword. A few hours later the unfortunate lady was there found dead by one of the castle servants, and the fear inspired by the room increased.

Poor Bluebeard, learning at one blow of his ample dishonour, and the tragic death of his wife, did not console himself for the latter misfortune by any consideration of the former. He had loved Blanche de Gibeaumex with a strange ardour, more dearly than he had loved Jeanne de La Cloche, Gigonne Traignel, or even Colette Passage. On learning that she had consistently betrayed him, and that now she would never betray him again, he experienced a grief and a mental perturbation which, far from being appeased, daily increased in violence. So intolerable were his sufferings that he contracted a malady which caused his life to be despaired of.

The physicians, having employed various medicines without effect, advised him that the only remedy proper to his complaint was to take a young wife. He then thought of his young cousin, Angèle de La Garandine, whom he believed would be willingly bestowed upon him, as she had no property. What encouraged him to take her to wife was the fact that she was reputed to be simple and ignorant of the world. Having been deceived by a woman of intelligence, he felt more comfortable with a fool. He married Mademoiselle de La Garandine, and quickly perceived the falsity of his calculations. Angèle was kind, Angèle was good, and Angèle loved him ; she had not, in herself, any leanings toward evil, but the least astute person could quickly lead her astray at any moment. It was enough to tell her : "Do this for fear of bogies; comes in here or the were-wolf will eat you;" or "Shut your eyes, and take this drop of medicine," and the innocent girl would straightway do so, at the will of the rascals who wanted of her that which it was very natural to want of her, for she was pretty. Monsieur de Montragoux, injured and betrayed by this innocent girl, as much as and more than he had been by Blanche de Gibeaumex, had the additional pain of knowing it, for Angèle was too candid to conceal anything from him. She used to tell him: "Sir, some one told me this; some one did that to me; some one took so and so away from me; I saw that; I felt so and so." And by her ingenuousness she caused her lord to suffer torments beyond imagination. He endured them like a Stoic. Still he finally had to tell the simple creature that she was a goose, and to box her ears. This, for him, was the beginning of a reputation for cruelty, which was not fated to be diminished. A mendicant monk, who was passing Guillettes while Monsieur de Montragoux was out shooting woodcock, found Madame Angèle sewing a doll's petticoat. This worthy friar, discovering that she was as foolish as she was beautiful, took her away on his donkey, having persuaded her that the Angel Gabriel was waiting in a wood, to give her a pair of pearl garters. It is believed that she must have been eaten by a wolf, for she was never seen again.

After such a disastrous experience, how was it that Bluebeard could make up his mind to contract yet another union? It would be impossible to understand it, were we not well aware of the power which a fine pair of eyes exerts over a generous heart.

The honest gentleman met, at a neighbouring château which he was in the habit of frequenting, a young orphan of quality, by name Alix de Pontalcin, who, having been robbed of all her property by a greedy trustee, thought only of entering a convent. Officious friends intervened to alter her determination and persuade her to accept the hand of Monsieur de Montragoux. Her beauty was perfect. Bluebeard, who was promising himself the enjoyment of an infinite happiness in her arms, was once more deluded in his hopes, and this time experienced a disappointment, which, owing to his disposition, was bound to make an even greater impression upon him than all the afflictions which he had suffered in his previous marriages. Alix de Pontalcin obstinately refused to give actuality to the union to which she had nevertheless consented.

In vain did Monsieur de Montragoux press her to become his wife; she resisted prayers, tears, and objurgations, she refused her husband's lightest caresses, and rushed off to shut herself into the Cabinet of the Unfortunate Princesses, where she remained, alone and intractable, for whole nights at a time.

The cause of a resistance so contrary to laws both human and divine was never known; it was attributed to Monsieur de Montragoux's blue beard, but our previous remarks on the subject of his beard render such a supposition far from probable. In any case, it is a difficult subject to discuss. The unhappy husband underwent the cruellest sufferings. In order to forget them, he hunted with desperation, exhausting horses, hounds, and huntsmen. But when he returned home, foundered and overtired, the mere sight of Mademoiselle de Pontalcin was enough to revive his energies and his torments. Finally, unable to endure the situation any longer, he applied to Rome for the annulment of a marriage which was nothing better than a trap; and in consideration of a handsome present to the Holy Father he obtained it in accordance with canon law. If Monsieur de Montragoux discarded Mademoiselle de Pontalcin with all the marks of respect due to a woman, and without breaking his cane across her back, it was because he had a valiant soul, a great heart, and was master of himself as well as of Guillettes. But he swore that, for the future, no female should enter his apartments. Happy had he been if he had held to his oath to the end!

CHAPTER III

SOME years had elapsed since Monsieur de Montragoux had rid himself of his sixth wife, and only a confused recollection remained in the country-side of the domestic calamities which had fallen upon this worthy *seigneur's* house. Nobody knew what had become of his wives, and hair-raising tales were told in the village at night; some believed them, others did not. About this time, a widow, past the prime of life, Dame Sidonie de Lespoisse, came to settle with her children in the manor of La Motte-Giron, about two leagues, as the crow flies, from the castle of Guillettes. Whence she came, or who her husband had been, not a soul knew. Some believed, because they had heard it said, that he had held certain posts in Savoy or Spain; others said that he had died in the Indies; many had the idea that the widow was possessed of immense estates, while others doubted it strongly. However, she lived in a notable style, and invited all the nobility of the country-side to La Motte-Giron. She had two daughters, of whom the elder, Anne, on the verge of becoming an old maid, was a very astute person: Jeanne, the younger, ripe for marriage, concealed a precocious knowledge of the world under an appearance of simplicity. The Dame de Lespoisse had also two sons, of twenty and twenty-two years of age; very fine well-made young fellows, of whom one was a Dragoon, and the other a Musketeer. I may add, having seen his commission, that he was a Black Musketeer. When on foot, this was not apparent, for the Black Musketeers were distinguished from the Grey not by the colour of their uniform, but by the hides of their horses. All alike wore blue surcoats laced with gold. As for the Dragoons, they were to be recognized by a kind of fur bonnet, of which the tail fell gallantly over the ear. The Dragoons had the reputation of being scamps, a scapegrace crowd, witness the song:

> "Mama, here the dragoons come:
> Let us haste away."

But you might have searched in vain through His Majesty's two regiments of Dragoons for a bigger rake, a more accomplished sponger, or a viler rogue than Cosme de Lespoisse. Compared with him, his brother was an honest lad. Drunkard and gambler, Pierre de Lespoisse pleased the ladies, and won at cards; these were the only ways of gaining a living known to him.

Their mother, Dame de Lespoisse, was making a splash at Motte-Giron only in order to catch gulls. As a matter of fact, she had not a penny, and owed for everything, even to her false teeth. Her clothes and furniture, her coach, her horses, and her servants had all been lent by Parisian money-lenders, who threatened to withdraw them all if she did not presently marry one of her daughters to some rich nobleman, and the respectable Sidonie was expecting to find herself at any moment naked in an empty house. In a hurry to find a son-in-law, she had at once cast her eye upon Monsieur de Montragoux, whom she summed up as being simple-minded, easy to deceive, extremely mild, and quick to fall in love under his rude and bashful exterior. Her two daughters entered into her plans, and every time they met him, riddled poor Bluebeard with glances which pierced him to the depths of his heart. He soon fell a victim to the potent charms of the two Demoiselles de Lespoisse. Forgetting his oath, he thought of nothing but marrying one of them, finding them equally beautiful. After some delay, caused less by hesitation than timidity, he went to Motte-Giron in great state, and made his petition to the Dame de Lespoisse, leaving to her the choice of which daughter she would give him. Madame Sidonie obligingly replied that she held him in high esteem, and that she authorized him to pay his court to whichever of the ladies he should prefer.

"Learn to please, monsieur," she said. "I shall be the first to applaud your success."

In order to make their better acquaintance, Bluebeard invited Anne and Jeanne de Lespoisse, with their mother, brothers, and a multitude of ladies and gentlemen to pass a fortnight at the castle of Guillettes. There was a succession of walking, hunting, and fishing parties, dances and festivities, dinners and entertainments of every sort. A young *seigneur*, the Chevalier de Merlus, whom the ladies Lespoisse had brought with them, organized the beats. Bluebeard had the best packs of hounds and the largest turnout in the countryside. The ladies rivalled the ardour of the gentlemen in hunting the deer. They did not always hunt the animal down, but the hunters and their ladies wandered away in couples, found one another, and again wandered off into the woods. For choice, the Chevalier de la Merlus would lose himself with Jeanne de Lespoisse, and both would return to the castle at night, full of their adventures, and pleased with their day's sport.

After a few days' observation, the good *seigneur* of Montragoux felt a decided preference for Jeanne, the younger sister, rather than the elder, as she was fresher, which is not saying that she was less experienced. He allowed his preference to appear; there was no reason why he should conceal it, for it was a befitting preference; moreover, he was a plain dealer. He paid court to the young lady as best he could, speaking little, for want of practice; but he gazed at her, rolling his rolling eyes, and emitting from the depths of his bowels sighs which might have overthrown an oak tree. Sometimes he would burst out laughing, whereupon the crockery trembled, and the windows rattled. Alone of all the party, he failed to remark the assiduous attentions of the Chevalier de la Merlus to Madame de Lespoisse's younger daughter, or if he did remark them he saw no harm in them. His experience of women was not sufficient to make him suspicious, and he trusted when he loved. My grandmother used to say that in life experience is worthless, and that one remains the same as when one begins. I believe she was right, and the true story that I am now unfolding is not of a nature to prove her wrong.

Bluebeard displayed an unusual magnificence in these festivities. When night arrived the lawns before the castle were lit by a thousand torches, and tables served by men-servants and maids dressed as fauns and dryads groaned under all the tastiest things which the country-side and the forest produced. Musicians provided a continual succession of beautiful symphonies. Towards the end of the meal the schoolmaster and schoolmistress, followed by the boys and girls of the village, appeared before the guests, and read a complimentary address to the *seigneur* of Montragoux and his friends. An astrologer in a pointed cap approached the ladies, and foretold their future love-affairs from the lines of their hands. Bluebeard ordered drink to be given for all his vassals, and he himself distributed bread and meat to the poor families.

At ten o'clock, for fear of the evening dew, the company retired to the apartments, lit by a multitude of candles, and there tables were prepared for every sort of game: lansquenet, billiards, reversi, bagatelle, pigeon-holes, turnstile, porch, beast, hoca, brelan, draughts, backgammon, dice, basset, and calbas. Bluebeard was uniformly unfortunate in these various games, at which he lost large sums every night. He could console himself for his continuous run of bad luck by watching the three Lespoisse ladies win a great deal of money. Jeanne, the younger, who often backed the game of the Chevalier de la Merlus, heaped up mountains of gold. Madame de Lespoisse's two sons also did very well at reversi and basset; their luck was invariably best at the more hazardous games. The play went on until late into the night. No one slept during these marvellous festivities, and as the earliest biographer of Bluebeard has said: "They spent the whole night in playing tricks on one another." These hours were the most delightful of the whole twenty-four; for then, under cover of jesting, and taking advantage of the darkness, those who felt drawn toward one another would hide together in the depths of some alcove. The Chevelier de la Merlus would disguise himself at one time as a devil, at another as a ghost or a were-wolf in order to frighten the sleepers, but he always ended by slipping into the room of Mademoiselle Jeanne de Lespoisse. The good *seigneur* of Montragoux was not overlooked in these games. The two sons of Madame de Lespoisse put irritant powder in his bed, and burnt in his room substances which emitted a disgusting smell. Or they would arrange a jug of water over his door so that the worthy *seigneur* could not open the door without the whole of the water being upset upon his head. In short, they played on him all sorts of practical jokes, to the diversion of the whole company, and Bluebeard bore them with his natural good humour.

He made his request, to which Madame de Lespoisse acceded, although, as she said, it wrung her heart to think of giving her girls in marriage.

The marriage was celebrated at Motte-Giron with extraordinary magnificence. The Demoiselle

Jeanne, amazingly beautiful, was dressed entirely in *point de France*, her head covered with a thousand ringlets. Her sister Anne wore a dress of green velvet, embroidered with gold. Their mother's dress was of golden tissue, trimmed with black chenille, with a *parure* of pearls and diamonds. Monsieur de Montragoux wore all his great diamonds on a suit of black velvet; he made a very fine appearance; his expression of timidity and innocence contrasting strongly with his blue chin and his massive build. The bride's brothers were of course handsomely arrayed, but the Chevalier de la Merlus, in a suit of rose velvet trimmed with pearls, shone with unparalleled splendour.

Immediately after the ceremony, the Jews who had hired out to the bride's family and her lover all these fine clothes and rich jewels resumed possession of them and posted back to Paris with them.

CHAPTER IV

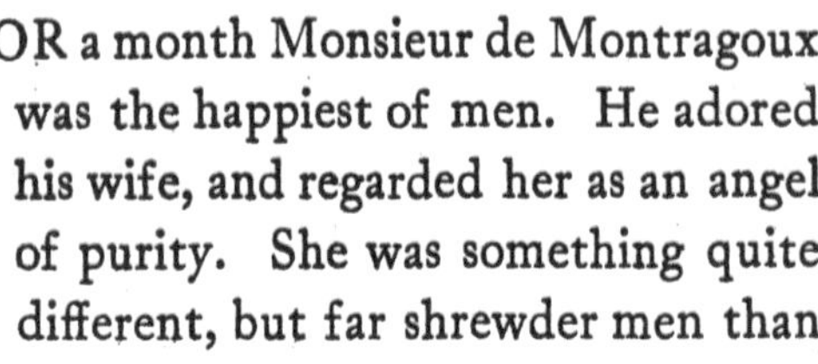

FOR a month Monsieur de Montragoux was the happiest of men. He adored his wife, and regarded her as an angel of purity. She was something quite different, but far shrewder men than poor Bluebeard might have been deceived as he was, for she was a person of great cunning and astuteness, and allowed herself submissively to be ruled by her mother, who was the cleverest jade in the whole kingdom of France. She established herself at Guillettes with her eldest daughter Anne, her two sons, Pierre and Cosme, and the Chevalier de la Merlus, who kept as close to Madame de Montragoux as if he had been her shadow. Her good husband was a little annoyed at this; he would have liked to keep his wife always to himself, but he did not take exception to the affection which she felt for this young gentleman, as she had told him that he was her foster-brother.

Charles Perrault relates that a month after having contracted this union, Bluebeard was compelled to make a journey of six weeks' duration on some important business. He does not seem to be aware of the reasons for this journey, and it has been suspected that it was an artifice, which the jealous husband resorted to, according to custom, in order to surprise his wife. The truth is quite otherwise. Monsieur de Montragoux went to Le Perche to receive the heritage of his cousin of Outarde, who had been killed gloriously by a cannon-ball at the battle of the Dunes, while casting dice upon a drum.

Before leaving, Monsieur de Montragoux begged his wife to indulge in every possible distraction during his absence.

" Invite all your friends, madame," he said, " go riding with them, amuse yourselves, and have a pleasant time."

He handed over to her all the keys of the house, thus indicating that in his absence she was the sole and sovereign mistress of all the *seigneurie* of Guillettes.

" This," he said, " is the key of the two great wardrobes ; this of the gold and silver not in daily use ; this of the strong-boxes which contain my gold and silver ; this of the caskets where my jewels are kept ; and this is a pass-key into all the rooms. As for this little key, it is that of the Cabinet, at the end of the Gallery, on the ground floor ; open everything, and go where you will."

Charles Perrault claims that Monsieur de Montragoux added :

" But as for the little Cabinet, I forbid you to enter that ; and I forbid you so expressly that if you do enter it, I cannot say to what lengths my anger will not go."

The historian of Bluebeard in placing these words on record, has fallen into the error of adopting, without verification, the version concocted after the event by the ladies Lespoisse. Monsieur de Montragoux expressed himself very differently. When he handed to his wife the key of the little Cabinet, which was none other than the Cabinet of the Unfortunate Princesses, to which we have already frequently alluded, he expressed the desire that his beloved Jeanne should not enter that part of the house which he regarded as fatal to his domestic happiness. It was through this room, indeed, that his first wife, and the best of all of them, had fled, when she ran away with her bear ; here Blanche de Gibeaumex had repeatedly betrayed him with various gentlemen ; and lastly, the porphyry pavement was stained by the blood of a beloved criminal. Was not this enough to make Monsieur de Montragoux connect the idea of this room with cruel memories and fateful forebodings ?

The words which he addressed to Jeanne de

Lespoisse convey the desires and impressions which were troubling his mind. They were actually as follows:

"For you, madame, nothing of mine is hidden, and I should feel that I was doing you an injury did I fail to hand over to you all the keys of a dwelling which belongs to you. You may therefore enter this little cabinet, as you may enter all the other rooms of the house; but if you will take my advice you will do nothing of the kind, to oblige me, and in consideration of the painful ideas which, for me, are connected with this room, and the forebodings of evil which these ideas, despite myself, call up into my mind. I should be inconsolable were any mischance to befall you, or were I to bring misfortune upon you. You will, madame, forgive these fears, which are happily unfounded, as being only the outcome of my anxious affection and my watchful love."

With these words the good *seigneur* embraced his wife and posted off to Le Perche.

"The friends and neighbours," says Charles Perrault, "did not wait to be asked to visit the young bride; so full were they of impatience to see all the wealth of her house. They proceeded at once to inspect all the rooms, cabinets, and wardrobes, each of which was richer and more beautiful than the last; and there was no end to their envy and their praises of their friend's good fortune."

All the historians who have dealt with this subject have added that Madame de Montragoux took no pleasure in the sight of all these riches, by reason of her impatience to open the little Cabinet. This is perfectly correct, and as Perrault has said: "So urgent was her curiosity that, without considering that it was unmannerly to leave her guests, she went down to it by a little secret staircase, and in such a hurry that two or three times she thought she would break her neck." The fact is beyond question. But what no one has told us is that the reason why she was so anxious to reach this apartment was that the Chevalier de la Merlus was awaiting her there.

Since she had come to make her home in the castle of Guillettes she had met this young gentleman in the Cabinet every day, and oftener twice a day than once, without wearying of an intercourse so unseemly in a young married woman. It is impossible to hesitate as to the nature of the ties connecting Jeanne with the Chevalier: they were anything but respectable, anything but chaste. Alas, had Madame de Montragoux merely betrayed her husband's honour, she would no doubt have incurred the blame of posterity; but the most austere of moralists might have found excuses for her. He might allege, in favour of so young a woman, the laxity of the morals of the period; the examples of the city and the Court; the too certain effects of a bad training, and the advice of an immoral mother, for Madame Sidonie de Lespoisse countenanced her daughter's intrigues. The wise might have forgiven her a fault too amiable to merit their severity; her errors would have seemed too common to be crimes, and the world would simply have considered that she was behaving like other people. But Jeanne de Lespoisse, not content with betraying her husband's honour, did not hesitate to attempt his life.

It was in the little Cabinet, otherwise known as the Cabinet of the Unfortunate Princesses, that Jeanne de Lespoisse, Dame de Montragoux, in concert with the Chevalier de la Merlus, plotted the death of a kind and faithful husband. She declared later that, on entering the room, she saw hanging there the bodies of six murdered women, whose congealed blood covered the tiles, and that recognizing in these unhappy women the first six wives of Bluebeard, she foresaw the fate which awaited herself. She must, in this case, have mistaken the paintings on the walls for mutilated corpses, and her hallucinations must be compared with those of Lady Macbeth. But it is extremely probable that Jeanne imagined this horrible sight in order to relate it afterwards, justifying her husband's murderers by slandering their victim.

The death of Monsieur de Montragoux was determined upon. Certain letters which lie before me compel the belief that Madame Sidonie Lespoisse had her part in the plot. As for her elder daughter, she may be described as the soul of the conspiracy. Anne de Lespoisse was the wickedest of the whole family. She was a stranger to sensual weakness, remaining chaste in the midst of the profligacy of the house; it was not a case of refusing pleasures which she thought unworthy of her; the truth was that she took pleasure only in cruelty. She engaged her two brothers, Cosme and Pierre, in the enterprise by promising them the command of a regiment.

CHAPTER V

T now rests with us to trace, with the aid of authentic documents, and reliable evidence, the most atrocious, treacherous, and cowardly domestic crime of which the record has come down to us. The murder whose circumstances we are about to relate can only be compared to that committed on the night of the 9th March, 1449, on the person of Guillaume de Flavy, by his wife Blanche d'Overbreuc, a young and slender woman, the bastard d'Orbandas, and the barber Jean Bocquillon. They stifled Guillaume with a pillow, battered him pitilessly with a club, and bled him at the throat like a calf. Blanche d'Overbreuc proved that her husband had determined to have her drowned, while Jeanne de Lespoisse betrayed a loving husband to a gang of unspeakable scoundrels. We will record the facts with all possible restraint.

Bluebeard returned rather earlier than expected. This it was gave rise to the quite mistaken idea that, a prey to the blackest jealousy, he was wishful to surprise his wife. Full of joy and confidence, if he thought of giving her a surprise it was an agreeable one. His kindness and tenderness, and his joyous, peaceable air would have softened the most savage hearts. The Chevalier de la Merlus, and the whole execrable brood of Lespoisse saw therein nothing but an additional facility for taking his life, and possessing themselves of his wealth, still further increased by his new inheritance.

His young wife met him with a smiling face, allowing herself to be embraced and led to the conjugal chamber, where she did everything to please the good man. The following morning she returned him the bunch of keys which had been confided to her care. But there was missing that of the Cabinet of the Unfortunate Princesses, commonly called the little Cabinet. Bluebeard gently demanded its delivery, and after putting him off for a time on various pretexts Jeanne returned it to him

There now arises a question which cannot be solved without leaving the limited domain of history to enter the indeterminate regions of philosophy.

Charles Perrault specifically states that the key of the little Cabinet was a fairy key, that is to say, it was magical, enchanted, endowed with properties contrary to the laws of nature, at all events, as we conceive them. We have no proof to the contrary. This is a fitting moment to recall the precept of my illustrious master, Monsieur du Clos des Lunes, a member of the Institute: "When the supernatural makes its appearance, it must not be rejected by the historian." I shall therefore content myself with recalling as regards this key, the unanimous opinion of all the old biographers of Bluebeard; they all affirm that it was a fairy key. This is a point of great importance. Moreover, this key is not the only object created by human industry which has proved to be endowed with marvellous properties. Tradition abounds with examples of enchanted swords. Arthur's was a magic sword. And so was that of Joan of Arc, on the undeniable authority of Jean Chartier; and the proof afforded by that illustrious chronicler is that when the blade was broken the two pieces refused to be welded together again despite all the efforts of the most competent armourers. Victor Hugo speaks in one of his poems of those "magic stairways still obscured below." Many authors even admit that there are men-magicians who can turn themselves into wolves. We shall not undertake to combat such a firm and constant belief, and we shall not pretend to decide whether the key of the little Cabinet was or was not enchanted, for our reserve does not imply that we are in any uncertainty, and therein resides its merit. But where we find ourselves in our proper domain, or to be more precise within our own jurisdiction, where we once more become judges of facts, and writers of circumstances, is where we read that the key was flecked with blood. The authority of the texts does not so far impress us as to compel us to believe this. It was not flecked with blood. Blood had flowed in the little cabinet, but at a time already remote. Whether the key had been washed or whether it had dried, it was impossible that it should be so stained, and what, in her agitation, the criminal wife mistook for a blood-stain on the iron, was the reflection of the sky still empurpled by the roses of dawn.

Monsieur de Montragoux, on seeing the key, perceived none the less that his wife had entered the little cabinet. He noticed that it now appeared cleaner and brighter than when he had given it to her, and was of opinion that this polish could only come from use.

This produced a painful impression upon him, and he said to his wife, with a mournful smile:

"My darling, you have been into the little cabinet. May there result no grievous outcome for either of us! From that room emanates a malign influence from which I would have protected you. If you, in your turn should become subjected to it, I should never get over it. Forgive me; when we love we are superstitious."

On these words, although Bluebeard cannot

have frightened her, for his words and demeanour expressed only love and melancholy, the young lady of Montragoux began shrieking at the top of her voice :

" Help ! Help ! he's killing me ! "

This was the signal agreed upon. On hearing it, the Chevalier de la Merlus and the two sons of Madame de Lespoisse were to have thrown themselves upon Bluebeard and run him through with their swords.

But the Chevalier, whom Jeanne had hidden in a cupboard in the room, appeared alone. Monsieur de Montragoux, seeing him leap forth sword in hand, placed himself on guard. Jeanne fled terror-stricken, and met her sister Anne in the gallery. She was not, as has been related, on a tower ; for all the towers had been thrown down by order of Cardinal Richelieu. Anne was striving to put heart into her two brothers, who, pale and quaking, dared not risk so great a stake.

Jeanne hastily implored them :

" Quick, quick, brothers, save my lover ! "

Pierre and Cosme then rushed at Bluebeard. They found him, having disarmed the Chevalier de la Merlus, holding him down with his knee ; they treacherously ran their swords through his body from behind, and continued to strike at him long after he had breathed his last.

Bluebeard had no heirs. His wife remained mistress of his property. She used a part of it to provide a dowry for her sister Anne, another part to buy captains' commissions for her two brothers, and the rest to marry the Chevalier de la Merlus, who became a very respectable man as soon as he was wealthy.

THE MIRACLE OF THE GREAT ST. NICOLAS

THE MIRACLE OF THE GREAT ST. NICOLAS

T. NICOLAS, Bishop of Myra in Lycia, lived in the time of Constantine the Great. The most ancient and weighty of those authors who have mentioned him celebrate his virtues, his labours, and his worth: they give abundant proofs of his sanctity; but none of them records the miracle of the salting-tub. Nor is it mentioned in the Golden Legend. This silence is important: still one does not willingly consent to throw doubt upon a fact so widely known, which is attested by the ballad which all the world knows:

> "There were three little children
> In the fields they went to glean."

This famous text expressly states that a cruel pork-butcher put the innocents "like pigs into the salting-vat." That is to say, he apparently preserved them, cut into pieces, in a bath of brine. This is, to be sure, how pork is cured: but one is surprised to read further on that the three little children remained seven years in pickle, whereas it is usual to begin withdrawing the pieces of flesh from the tub, with a wooden fork, at the end of about six weeks. The text is explicit: according to the elegy, it was seven years after the crime that St. Nicolas entered the accursed hostelry. He asked for supper. The landlord offered him a piece of ham:

"'Wilt eat of ham? 'Tis dainty food.'
'I'll have no ham: it is not good.'
'Wilt eat a piece of tender veal?'
'I will not make of that my meal.
Young salted flesh I want, and that
Has lain seven years within the vat.'
Whenas the butcher heard this said
Out of the door full fast he fled."

The Man of God immediately resuscitated the tender victims by the laying of hands on the salting-tub.

Such is, in substance, the story of the old anonymous rhyme. It bears the inimitable stamp of honesty and good faith. Scepticism seems ill-inspired when it attacks the most vital memories of the popular mind. It is not without a lively satisfaction that I have found myself able to reconcile the authority of the ballad with the silence of the ancient biographers of the Lycian pontiff. I am happy to proclaim the result of my long meditations and scholastic researches. The miracle of the salting-tub is true, in so far as essentials are concerned, but it was not the blessed Bishop of Myra who performed it; it was another St. Nicolas, for there were two: one, as we have already stated, Bishop of Myra in Lycia; the other more recent, Bishop of Trinqueballe in Vervignole. For me was reserved the task of distinguishing between them. It was the Bishop of Trinqueballe who rescued the three little boys from the salting-tub. I shall establish the fact by authentic documents, and no one will have occasion to deplore the end of a legend.

I have been fortunate enough to recover the entire history of the Bishop Nicolas and the children whom he resuscitated. I have fashioned it into in a narrative which will be read, I hope, with both pleasure and profit.

CHAPTER I

NICOLAS, a scion of an illustrious family of Vervignole, showed marks of sanctity from his earliest childhood, and at the age of fourteen vowed to consecrate himself to the Lord. Having embraced the ecclesiastical profession, he was raised, while still young, by popular acclamation and the wish of the Chapter, to the see of St. Cromadaire, the apostle of Vervignole, and first Bishop of Trinqueballe. He exercised his pastoral ministry with piety, governed his clergy with wisdom, taught the people, and feared not to remind the great of Justice and Moderation. He was liberal, profuse in almsgiving, and set aside for the poor the greater part of his wealth.

His castle proudly lifted its crenelated walls and pepper-pot roofs from the summit of a hill overlooking the town. He made of it a refuge where all who were pursued by the secular arm might find a place of refuge. In the lower hall, the largest to be seen in all Vervignole, the table laid for meals was so long that those who sat at one end saw it lose itself in the distance in an indistinct point, and when the torches upon it were lighted it recalled the tail of the comet which appeared in Vervignole to announce the death of King Comus. The holy St. Nicolas sat at the upper end. There he entertained the principal folk of the town and of the kingdom, and a multitude of clergy and laymen. But on his right there was always reserved a seat for the poor man who might come begging for his bread at the door.

Children, particularly, aroused the solicitude of the good St. Nicolas. He delighted in their innocence, and he felt for them with the heart of a father and the bowels of a mother. He had the virtues and the morals of an apostle. Yearly, in the dress of a simple monk, with a white staff in his hand, he would visit his flock, desirous of seeing everything with his own eyes; and in order that no adversity or disorder should escape his notice he would traverse, accompanied by a single priest, the wildest parts of his diocese, crossing, in winter, the flooded rivers, climbing mountains, and plunging into the thick forests.

One day, having ridden since dawn upon his mule, in company with the Deacon Modernus, through gloomy woods haunted by the lynx and the wolf, and the ancient pines bristling on the summits of the Marnouse mountains, the man of God made his way at the fall of night into some thorny thickets through which his mount with difficulty forced a winding path. The Deacon Modernus followed him with much difficulty on his mule, which carried the baggage.

Overcome with hunger and fatigue, the man of God said to Modernus:

"Let us halt here, my son, and if you still have a little bread and wine we will sup here, for I feel that I hardly have the strength to proceed further, and you, although the younger, must be nearly as tired as I."

"Monseigneur," answered Modernus, "there remains neither a drop of wine nor a crumb of bread; for, by your orders, I gave all to some people on the road, who had less need of it than ourselves."

"Without a doubt," replied the Bishop, "had there been a few scraps left in your wallet we should have eaten them with pleasure, for it is fitting that those who govern the Church should be nourished on the leavings of the poor. But since you have nothing left it is because God has desired it so, and He has surely desired it for our good and profit. It is possible that He will for ever hide from us the reason of this favour: perhaps, on the other hand, He will quickly make it manifest. Meanwhile, I think the only thing left for us is to push on until we find some arbutus berries and blackberries for our own nourishment, and some grass for our mules, and, being thus refreshed, to lie down upon a bed of leaves."

"As you please, Monseigneur," answered Modernus, pricking his mount.

They travelled all night, and a part of the following morning; then, having climbed a fairly steep ascent, they suddenly found themselves at the border of the wood, and beheld at their feet a plain covered by a yellowish sky, and crossed by four white roads, which lost themselves in the mist. They took that to the left, an old Roman road, formerly frequented by merchants and pilgrims, but deserted since the war had laid waste this part of Vervignole. Dense clouds were gathering in the sky, across which birds were flying; a stifling atmosphere weighed down upon the dumb, livid earth. Lightning flashed on the horizon. They urged on their wearied mules. Suddenly a mighty wind bent the tops of the trees, making the boughs crack and the battered foliage moan. The thunder muttered, and heavy drops of rain began to fall.

As they made their way through the storm, the lightning flashing about them, along a road which had become a torrent, they perceived, by the light of a flash, a house outside which there hung a branch of holly, the sign of hospitality.

The inn appeared deserted; nevertheless, the host advanced towards them, a man fierce yet humble, with a great knife at his belt, and asked what they wished for.

"A lodging, and a scrap of bread, with a drop of wine," answered the Bishop, "for we are weary and benumbed with cold."

While the host was fetching wine from the cellar, and Modernus was taking the mules to the stable, St. Nicolas, sitting at the hearth beside a dying fire, cast a glance round the smoky room. Dust and dirt covered the benches and casks; spiders spun their webs between the worm-eaten joists, whence hung scanty bunches of onions. In a dark corner the salting-tub displayed its iron-hooped belly.

In those days the demons used to take a hand in domestic life in a far more intimate fashion than they do to-day. They haunted houses, concealed in the salt-box, the butter-tub, or some other hiding-place; they spied upon the people of the house, and watched for the opportunity to tempt them and lead them into evil. Then, too, the angels made more frequent appearances among Christian folk.

Now a devil, as big as a hazel-nut, who was hidden among the burning logs, spoke up and said to the holy Bishop:

"Look at that salting-tub, Father; it is well worth a look. It is the best salting-tub in the whole of Vervignole. It is, indeed, the model and paragon of salting-tubs. When the master here, Seigneur Garum, received it from the hands of a skilful cooper he perfumed it with juniper, thyme, and rosemary. Seigneur Garum has not his equal in bleeding the meat, boning it, and cutting it up, carefully, thoughtfully, and lovingly, and steeping it in salted liquors by which it is preserved and embalmed. He is without a rival for seasoning, concentrating, boiling down, skimming, straining, and decanting the pickle. Taste his mild-cured pork, father, and you will lick your fingers: taste his mild-cured pork, Nicolas, and you will have something to say about it."

But in these words, and above all in the voice that uttered them (it grated like a saw), the holy Bishop recognized an evil spirit. He made the sign of the Cross, whereupon the little devil exploded with a horrible noise and a very bad smell, just like a chestnut thrown into the fire without having had its skin split.

And an angel from Heaven appeared, resplendent in light and said to Nicolas:

"Nicolas, beloved of the Lord, you must know that three little children have been in that salting-tub for seven years; Garum, the innkeeper, cut up these tender infants, and put them in salt and pickle. Arise, Nicolas, and pray that they may come to life again. For, if you intercede for them, O Pontiff, the Lord, who loves you, will restore them to life."

During this speech Modernus entered the room, but he did not see the angel, nor did he hear him, for he was not sufficiently holy to be able to communicate with the heavenly spirits.

The angel further said:

"Nicolas, son of God, lay your hands on the salting-tub, and the three children will be resuscitated."

The blessed Nicolas, filled with horror, pity, zeal, and hope, gave thanks to God, and when the innkeeper reappeared with a jug in either hand, the Saint said to him in a terrible voice:

"Garum, open the salting-tub!"

Whereupon, Garum, overcome by fear, dropped both his jugs.

And the saintly Bishop Nicolas stretched out his hands, and said:

"Children, arise!"

At these words, the lid of the salting-tub was lifted up, and three young boys emerged.

"Children," said the Bishop, "give thanks to God, who through me, has raised you from out the salting-tub."

And turning towards the innkeeper, who was trembling in every limb, he said :

" Cruel man, recognize the three children whom you shamefully put to death. May you loathe your crime, and repent, that God may pardon you ! "

The innkeeper, filled with terror, fled into the storm, amidst the thunder and lightning.

CHAPTER II

ST. NICOLAS embraced the three children and gently questioned them about the miserable death which they had suffered. They related that Garum, having approached them while they were gleaning in the fields, had lured them into his inn, had made them drink wine, and had cut their throats while they slept.

They still wore the rags in which they had been clothed on the day of their death, and they retained, after their resurrection, a wild and timid air. The sturdiest of the three, Maxime, was the son of a half-witted woman, who followed the soldiers to war, mounted on an ass. One night he fell from the pannier in which she carried him, and was left abandoned by the roadside. From that time forward he had lived solely by theft. The feeblest, Robin, could hardly recall his parents, peasants in the highlands, who being too poor or too avaricious to support him had deserted him in the forest. The third, Sulpice, knew nothing of his birth, but a priest had taught him his alphabet.

The storm had ceased; in the buoyant, limpid

air the birds were calling loudly to one another. The smiling earth was green. Modernus having fetched the mules, Bishop Nicolas mounted his, and carried Maxime wrapped in his cloak: the deacon took Sulpice and Robin upon his crupper, and they set off toward the city of Trinqueballe.

The road unfolded itself between fields of corn, vineyards, and meadows. As they went along the great Saint Nicolas who already loved the children with all his heart, examined them on subjects suitable to their age, and asked them easy questions such as: "How much is five times five?" or "What is God?" He obtained no satisfactory answers. But, far from shaming them for their ignorance, he thought only of gradually dissipating it by the application of the best pedagogic methods.

"Modernus," he said, "we will teach them firstly the truths necessary for salvation, and secondly the liberal arts, especially music, so that they may sing the praises of the Lord. It will also be expedient to teach them rhetoric, philosophy, and the history of men, plants, and animals. I desire that they shall study, in their habits and their structure, the animals, all of whose organs, in their wonderful perfection, attest the glory of the Creator."

Scarcely had the venerable Pontiff concluded this speech when a peasant woman passed along the road, dragging by the halter an old mare so heavily laden with branches cut with their leaves on that her knees were trembling, and she stumbled at every step.

"Alas," sighed the great St. Nicolas, "here is a poor horse carrying more than its burden. He has unfortunately fallen into the hands of unjust and hard-hearted masters. One should not overload any creature, not even beasts of burden."

At these words the three boys burst out laughing. The Bishop having asked why they laughed so loudly:

"Because——" said Robin.

"That is——" said Sulpice.

"We laughed," said Maxime, "because you mistook a mare for a horse. Can't you see the difference? It is very plain to me. Don't you know anything about animals?"

"I think," said Modernus, "the first thing is to teach these children manners."

At every town, borough, village, hamlet or castle by which he passed, St. Nicolas showed the people the children rescued from the salting-tub, and related the great miracle performed by God, on his intercession; whereupon they were all very joyful, and blessed him. Informed by messengers and travellers of so prodigious an occurrence, the entire population of Trinqueballe came out to meet their pastor, unrolling precious carpets and scattering flowers in his path. The citizens, their eyes wet with tears, gazed at the three victims who had escaped from the salting-tub, and cried: "The Lord be praised!" But the poor children knew no better than to laugh and stick out their tongues; this caused further wonder and compassion, as being a palpable proof of their innocence and misfortune.

The saintly Bishop Nicolas had an orphan niece, Mirande by name, who had just reached her seventh year, and was dearer to him than the light of his eyes. A worthy widow by name Basine was rearing her in piety, good manners, and ignorance of evil. The three miraculously saved children were confided to the care of this lady. She was not lacking in judgment. She quickly saw that Maxime had courage, Robin prudence, and Sulpice the power of reflection. She devoted herself to confirming these good qualities, which, by the corruption common to the whole human race, tended unceasingly to become perverted and distorted; for Robin's cautiousness turned easily into hypocrisy, and mostly hid a greedy covetousness; Maxime was subject to fits of rage, and Sulpice frequently and obstinately expressed false ideas in very important matters. However, they were but mere children who went bird's-nesting, stole the garden fruit, tied cooking-pots to dogs' tails, put ink the holy water font, and cow-itch in Modernus' bed.

At night, wrapped in white sheets and walking on stilts, they would go into the gardens, and frighten into a swoon the serving-maids belated in their lovers' arms. They would cover the seat which Madame Basine was wont to use with bristling spikes, and when she sat down they would delight in her sufferings, observing the confusion with which she openly applied a heedful and comforting hand to the damaged spot, for she would not for all the world have been lacking in modesty.

In spite of her age and virtues, this lady inspired them with neither love nor fear. Robin called her an old goat, Maxime an old she-ass, and Sulpice, the ass of Balaam. They teased little Mirande in all sorts of ways; they would dirty her pretty clothes by making her fall face downward on the stones. Once they pushed her head right up to the neck into a barrel of treacle. They taught her to sit astride railings, and to climb trees, contrary to the decorum of her sex; they taught her words and manners that smacked of the inn and the salting-tub. Following their example, she called Madame Bassne " an old goat," and even, taking the part for the whole, "old goat's rump." But she remained completely innocent. The purity of her soul was unchangeable.

"I am fortunate," said the holy Bishop Nicolas, "in that I rescued these children from the salting-tub, to make them good Christians. They will become faithful servants of God, and their merits will be accounted to me."

Now, by the third year after their resurrection, when they were already tall and well-made, on a day of spring, as they were all playing in the field beside the river, Maxime in a moment of facetiousness and natural high spirits, threw the Deacon Modernus into the water. Hanging on to the branch of a willow-tree, Modernus called for help. Robin ran up, made as though to draw him out by the hand, took off his ring, and fled.

Meanwhile, Sulpice, sitting motionless on the bank with his arms crossed, said:

"Modernus is making a bad end. I can see six devils, in the form of flittermice, ready to seize his soul as it comes out of his mouth."

When this serious affair was reported to him by Madame Basine and Modernus, the holy Bishop was much afflicted and fell a-sighing.

"These children," he said, "were reared in suffering, by unworthy parents. The excess of their misfortunes has caused the deformity of their characters. We must redress their wrongs by enduring patience, and persevering kindness."

"Monseigneur," answered Modernus, who was chattering with fever in his dressing-gown, and sneezing under his nightcap, for his bath had given him a cold, "it is possible that their wickedness is derived from the wickedness of their parents. But how do you explain, father, the fact that neglect has produced in each of them different and, so to speak, contrary vices, and that the desertion and destitution into which they were thrown before they were put in the salting-tub has made one avaricious, a second violent, and the third a visionary? And in your place, my Lord, I should feel most uneasy about the last."

"Each of these children," answered the Bishop, "has yielded in his weak spot. Ill-treatment has deformed their souls in those portions that offered the least resistance. Let us straighten them out with a thousand precautions, for fear of increasing the evil instead of diminishing it. Mildness, clemency, and forbearance are the only means which should ever be employed for the improvement of men, heretics of course excepted."

"No doubt, Monseigneur, no doubt," said Modernus, sneezing three times. "But you cannot have a good education without chastisement, nor discipline without discipline. I know what I am about. If you do not punish these three little ragamuffins, they will grow up worse than Herod. I assure you I am right."

"Modernus could not be mistaken," said Madame Basine.

The Bishop did not answer. With the widow and the Deacon, he paced the length of a hawthorn hedge, which breathed forth an agreeable fragrance of honey and bitter almonds. In a slight hollow, where the soil received the water from a neighbouring spring, he stopped before a bush, whose twisted, close-packed branches were covered with gleaming, clean-cut leaves and white clusters of flowers.

"Look," he said, "at this leafy, fragrant shrub, this lovely may, this noble thorn-bush, so strong and vigorous. Observe that it is in more abundant leaf, and more glorious with bloom, than all the other thorns in the hedge. But notice also that the pale bark of its branches bears only a few thorns, which are weak and soft and blunt. What is the reason of this? It is because, growing in a rich, moist soil, quiet and secure in the wealth which sustains its life, it has utilized all the juices of the earth to augment its power and its glory, and being too strong to dream of arming against its feeble enemies, it has devoted itself entirely to the joys of its magnificent and delicious fertility. Now come a few steps up this rising path, and look at this other hawthorn, which having with difficulty issued from a dry, stony soil, languishes, deficient in both wood and leaves, and has had no other thought during its hard life than to defend itself against the innumerable enemies that threaten the weak. It is nothing but a bundle of thorns. It has employed the little sap which it received in fashioning innumerable spears, broad at the base, hard and sharp, which but ill restore confidence to its apprehensive weakness. It has nothing left over for fruitful and fragrant blossom. My friends, we are like the hawthorns. The care given to our childhood makes us better. Too harsh an upbringing hardens us."

CHAPTER III

HEN Maxime was approaching his seventeenth year he filled the holy Bishop Nicolas with grief and the diocese with scandal by forming and training a company of rogues of his own age, with a view to kidnapping the girls of a village called Grosses-Nates, situated at a distance of four leagues from Trinqueballe. The expedition was marvellously successful. The ravishers entered the village by night, clasping to their bosoms the dishevelled virgins, who vainly uplifted to heaven their burning eyes and imploring hands. But when the fathers, brothers, and betrothed of these ravished maidens sought them out, they refused to return to the place of their birth, alleging that they felt too deeply shamed, and preferred to hide their dishonour in the arms that had caused it. Maxime, who, for his share, had taken the three most beautiful, was living in their company in a little manor dependent upon the episcopal See. In the absence of their ravisher, the Deacon Modernus arrived, by order of the Bishop, to knock at their door, answering that he came to set them free. They refused to open; and when he represented to them the abomination of their lives they dropped upon his head a crockful of dish-water, with the crock, by which his skull was fractured.

Armed with a gentle severity, the holy Bishop reproached Maxime for this violence and disorder:

"Alas," he said, "did I draw you from out of the salting-box to the ruin of the virgins of Vervignole?"

And he reproached him with the magnitude of his offence. But Maxime shrugged his shoulders, and turned his back, without making any reply.

At that moment King Berlu, in the fourteenth year of his reign, was assembling a powerful army to fight the Mambournians, the determined enemies of his kingdom, who, having entered Vervignole, were ravaging and depopulating the richest provinces of that great country.

Maxime left Trinqueballe without saying good-bye to a soul. When he was some leagues distant from the town, seeing in a field a mare of moderate quality, except that she was blind in one eye and lame, he jumped on her back and galloped off. On the following morning, accidentally meeting a farm lad who was taking a great plough horse to water, he immediately dismounted, bestrode the great horse, and ordered the lad to mount the blind mare, and to follow him, saying that he would take him for his squire should he prove satisfactory. Thus equipped Maxime presented himself to King Berlu, who accepted his services. He became in a very short time one of Vervignole's greatest captains.

Meanwhile, Sulpice was giving the holy Bishop cause for perhaps more cruel, and certainly more momentous, uneasiness; for if Maxime sinned grievously, he sinned without malice, and offending God without thought, and, so to speak, unknowingly. But Sulpice set himself to do evil with a greater and more unusual malignity. Being destined from early youth for the Church he assiduously studied letters, both sacred and profane; but his soul was a corrupted vessel, wherein Truth was turned into Error. He sinned in spirit; he erred in matters of faith with surprising precocity. At an age when people have as yet no ideas at all, he overflowed with wrong ones. A thought occurred to him which was doubtless suggested by the devil. In a field belonging to the Bishop he gathered a multitude of boys and girls of his own age and, climbing into a tree, he exhorted them to leave their fathers and mothers to follow Jesus Christ, and to go in parties through the country-side, burning priories and presbyteries in order to lead the Church back into evangelical poverty. This youthful mob, led away by emotion, followed the sinner along the roads of Vervignole, singing canticles, burning barns, pillaging chapels, and devastating the ecclesiastical lands. Many of these crazy creatures perished of fatigue, hunger, and cold, or were killed by villagers. The episcopal palace re-echoed with the complaints of the priesthood and the lamentations of mothers.

The pious Bishop Nicolas sent for the originator of these disorders. With extreme mildness, and infinite sadness, he reproached him for having misused the Word for the misleading of souls, and reminded him that God had not picked him out of the salting-tub in order that he should attack the property of our Holy Mother, the Church.

"Consider, my son," he said, "the greatness of your offence. You appear before your pastor charged with turmoil, sedition, and murder."

But young Sulpice, maintaining a horrid calm, answered with a voice full of assurance, that he had not sinned, neither had he offended God; but, on the contrary, he had acted in accordance with the bidding of Heaven, for the good of the Church. And he professed before the dismayed Bishop the false doctrines of the Manicheans, the Arians, the Nestorians, the Sabellians, the Vaudois, the Albigenses, and the Bégards. So eager was he to embrace these monstrous errors that he did not see how they contradicted one another, and were mutually devoured in the bosom that cherished and revived them.

The pious Bishop endeavoured to lead Sulpice back into the right path, but he failed to overcome the unhappy lad's obstinacy.

Having dismissed him, he knelt and prayed.

" I thank thee, O Lord, for having sent me this young man, as a whetstone on which to sharpen my patience and my charity."

While two of the children he had rescued from the salting-tub were causing him so much pain, St. Nicolas was obtaining some consolation from the third. Robin showed himself neither violent in his actions nor arrogant in his thoughts. He had not the sturdy, ruddy appearance of Maxime ; nor the grave, audacious manner of Sulpice. Small, thin, yellow, lined, and shrunken, of humble, obsequious and reverential bearing, he devoted himself to assisting the Bishop and clergy, helping the clerks to keep the accounts of the episcopal revenues, and making complicated calculations with the assistance of balls threaded on rods ; he even multiplied and divided numbers in his head, without the use of slate or pencil, with a rapidity and accuracy that would have been admired even in a past master of money and finance. For him it was a pleasure to keep the books of the Deacon Modernus, who, growing old, used to muddle the figures and fall asleep at his desk. To oblige the Bishop, and obtain money for him, he spared neither trouble nor fatigue. From the Lombards, he learnt how to calculate both the simple and compound interest on a sum of money for a day, week, month, or year; he feared not to visit the filthy Jews in the black lanes of the Ghetto, in order to learn, by mingling with them, the standard of metals, the price of precious stones, and the art of clipping coin. Ultimately, with a little store which he had accumulated by marvellous industry in Vervignole, in Mondousiana, and even in Mambournia, he attended the fairs, tournaments, pardons, and jubilees, to which people of all conditions flocked from all parts of Christendom: peasants, burghers, clerics, and *seigneurs;* there he changed their money, and every time he returned a little richer than he had departed. Robin did not spend the money he had made, but brought it to the Bishop.

St. Nicolas was extremely hospitable, and very liberal in almsgiving. He spent all his property and that of the Church in making gifts to pilgrims and assisting the unfortunate. Thus he continually found himself short of money; and he was much obliged to Robin for the skill and energy with which the young treasurer obtained the sums which he required. The condition of penury in which the holy Bishop had placed himself owing to his magnificence and liberality was greatly aggravated by the condition of the times. The war which was ravaging Vervignole also ruined the Church in Trinqueballe. The soldiery who were fighting in the country-side about the town pillaged the farms, levied contributions on the peasantry, drove out the religious orders, and burned the castles and abbeys.

The clergy and the faithful could no longer contribute to the expenses of their creed, and thousands of peasants, fleeing from the free-booters came daily to beg their bread at the door of the episcopal palace. For their sakes, the good St. Nicolas felt the poverty which he had never felt for his own. Fortunately, Robin was always ready to lend him money, which the holy pontiff naturally agreed to return in more prosperous times.

Alas, the war was now raging throughout the kingdom, from north to south, from east to west, attended by its two inseparable companions, famine and pestilence. The peasantry turned robbers, and the monks followed the armies. The inhabitants of Trinqueballe, having neither wood for firing, nor bread to eat, died like flies at the approach of winter. Wolves entered the outlying parts of the town, devouring little children. At this sad juncture, Robin came to inform the Bishop that not only was he unable to provide any further sum of money, however small, but that being unable to obtain anything from his debtors, and being pressed by his creditors, he had been compelled to hand over all his assets to the Jews.

He brought this distressing news to his benefactor with the obsequious politeness which was usual to him; but he appeared a great deal less afflicted than he might have been in this grevious extremity. As a matter of fact, he was hard put to it to conceal, under a long face, his joyous feelings and his lively satisfaction. The parchment of his dry, humble, yellow eyelids ill concealed the light of joy which shone from his sharp eyes.

Sadly stricken, St. Nicolas remained quiet and serene under the blow.

"God will soon re-establish our declining affairs," he said. "He will not permit the house which He has built to be overthrown."

"That is true," said Modernus, "but you may be sure that Robin, whom you drew out of the salting-tub, has made an arrangement with the Lombards of Pont-Vieux and the Jews of the Ghetto to despoil you, and that he is retaining the lion's share of the plunder."

Modernus spoke the truth. Robin had lost no money. He was richer than ever, and had just been appointed treasurer to the King.

CHAPTER IV

AT this time Mirande was nearing the close of her seventeenth year. She was beautiful, and well grown. An air of purity, innocence, and artlessness hung round her like a veil. The length of her eyelashes, which barred her blue eyes, and the childlike smallness of her mouth, gave the impression that evil could never find means to enter into her. Her ears were so tiny, so fine, so finished and so delicate, that the least modest of men could never have dared to breathe into them any but the most innocent of speeches. In the whole of Vervignole no virgin inspired so much respect, and none had greater need to do so, for she was marvellously simple, credulous, and defenceless.

The pious Bishop Nicolas, her uncle, cherished her more dearly every day, and was more deeply attached to her than one should be to any of God's creatures. He loved her, undoubtedly, in God; but he also loved her for herself; he took great delight in her, and he loved to love her; it was his only weakness. The Saints themselves are not always able to cut through all the ties of the flesh.

St. Nicolas loved his niece, with a pure love, but not without gratification of the senses. On the day following that on which he had learned of Robin's bankruptcy, he went to see Mirande in order to hold pious converse with her, as was his duty, for he stood in the place of a father to her, and had taken charge of her education.

She lived in the upper town, near the Cathedral in a house called "The House of the Musicians," because there were to be seen on its front men and animals playing on divers instruments. There were, notably, an ass playing a flute, and a philosopher, recognizable by his long beard and ink-horn, clashing cymbals. Every one explained these figures according to his fancy. It was the finest dwelling-house in the town.

The Bishop found his niece crouching on the floor, with dishevelled hair, her eyes glittering with tears, by the side of an empty, open coffer, in a room full of confusion.

He inquired of her the reason of this affliction, and of the disorder that prevailed around her. Turning upon him her despairing gaze, she told him with a thousand sighs that Robin, the Robin who had escaped from the salting-tub, the darling Robin, having many a time told her that if she ever wanted a dress, an ornament or a jewel, he would gladly lend her the money wherewith to buy it, she had frequently had recourse to his kindness, which appeared inexhaustible; but that very morning a Jew called Seligmann had come to her with four sheriff's officers, had presented the notes, signed by herself, which she had given Robin, and as she had not the money to pay them he had taken away all the clothes, head-dresses and jewels which she possessed.

"He has taken," she sobbed, "my bodices and petticoats of velvet, brocade and lace; my diamonds, my emeralds, my sapphires, my jacinths, my amethysts, my rubies, my garnets, and my turquoises; he has taken my great diamond cross, with angels' heads in enamel, my large necklace, consisting of two table diamonds, three cabochons, and six knots each of four pearls; he has taken my great collar of thirteen table diamonds, and twenty hanging pearls!"

And without saying more she wept bitterly into her handkerchief.

"My daughter," answered the saintly Bishop, "a Christian virgin is sufficiently adorned when she wears modesty for a necklace, and chastity for a girdle. None the less, as the scion of a most noble and most illustrious family it was right that you should wear diamonds and pearls. Your jewels were the treasury of the poor, and I deplore the fact that they should have been snatched from you."

He assured her that she would certainly recover them, either in this world or the next; he said everything possible to assuage her regret, and soothe her sorrow, and he comforted her. For she had a tender soul, which longed for consolation. But he himself left her full of affliction.

On the following day, as he was about to celebrate Mass in the cathedral, the holy Bishop saw coming towards him, in the sacristy, the three Jews, Seligmann, Issachar, and Meyer, who, wearing green hats and fillets upon their shoulders, very humbly presented him the notes which Robin had made over to them. As the venerable pontiff could not pay them, they called up twenty porters, with baskets, sacks, picklocks, carts, cords, and ladders, and commenced to pick the locks of the wardrobes, coffers, and tabernacles. The holy man cast on them a look which would have destroyed three Christians. He threatened them with the penalties of sacrilege, both in this world and the next, he pointed out that their mere presence in the house of the God, whom they had crucified, called down the fire of heaven upon their heads. They listened with the calm of people for whom anathema, reprobation, malediction, and execration were their daily bread. He then prayed to them, besought them, and promised to pay as soon as he could, twofold, threefold, tenfold, a hundredfold, the debt which they had acquired. They excused themselves politely for being unable to postpone the little transaction. The Bishop threatened to sound the tocsin, to rouse against them the people who would kill them like dogs for profaning, violating, and stealing the miraculous images and holy relics. They smilingly pointed to the sheriff's officers, who were guarding them. They were protected by King Berlu, for they lent him money.

At this sight the holy Bishop, recognizing that resistance would be rebellion, and remembering Him who replaced the ear of Malchus, remained inert and speechless, and bitter tears dropped from his eyes. Seligmann, Issachar, and Meyer took away the golden shrines enriched with precious stones, enamels and cabochons, the reliquaries in the form of chalices, lanterns, naves, and towers, the portable altars of alabaster encased in gold and silver, the coffers enamelled by the skilful craftsmen of Limoges and the Rhine, the altar-crosses, the Gospels bound in carved ivory and antique cameos, the desks ornamented with festoons of trailing vines, the consular registers, the pyxes, the candelabra and candlesticks, the lamp, of which they blew out the sacred flame, and spilt the blessed oil on the tiles, the chandeliers like enormous crowns, the chaplets with beads of pearl and amber, the eucharistic doves, the ciboria, the chalices, the patens, the kisses of peace, incense boxes and flagons, the innumerable ex-votos—hands, arms, legs, eyes, mouths, and hearts, all of silver—the nose of King Sidoc, the breast of Queen Blandine, and the head in solid gold of Saint Cromadaire, the first apostle of Vervignole, and the blessed patron of Trinqueballe. They even carried off the miraculous image of St. Gibbosine, whom the people of Vervignole had never invoked in vain in time of pestilence, famine, or war. This very ancient and venerable image was made of leaves of beaten gold nailed upon a core of cedar-wood, and was covered with precious stones of the bigness of ducks' eggs, which emitted fiery rays of red, blue, yellow and violet and white. For the past three hundred years her enamelled eyes, wide open in her golden face, had compelled such respect from the inhabitants of Trinqueballe that they saw her in their dreams, splendid and terrible, threatening them with the direst penalties if they failed to supply her with sufficient quantities of virgin wax and crown-pieces. St. Gibbosine groaned, trembled, and tottered on her pedestal, and allowed herself to be carried away without resistance, out of the basilica to which, from time immemorial, she had drawn innumerable pilgrims.

After the departure of these sacrilegious thieves the holy Bishop Nicolas ascended the steps of the despoiled altar, and consecrated the blood of our Lord in an old silver chalice, of German origin, thin and deeply dented. He prayed for the afflicted, and in particular for Robin, whom, by the will of God, he had rescued from the salting-box.

CHAPTER V

SHORTLY after this, King Berlu defeated the Mambournians in a great battle. He was, at first, unaware of the fact, for armed conflicts always present a great confusion, and during the last two hundred years the Vervignolians had lost the habit of victory. But the precipitate and disordered flight of the Mambournians informed him of his advantage. Instead of fighting a rear-guard action he pursued the enemy, and regained half his kingdom. The victorious army entered the city of Trinqueballe, all beflagged and beflowered in its honour, and in that illustrious capital of Vervignole it committed a great number of rapes, thefts, murders, and other cruelties, burnt several houses, sacked the churches, and took from the cathedral all that the Jews had left there, which, truth to tell, was not much.

Maxime, who having become a knight and commander of eighty lances, had largely contributed to the victory, was one of the first to enter the city, and repaired straightway to the House of the Musicians, where dwelt the beautiful Mirande, whom he had not seen since his departure for the war. He found her in her bower, plying her distaff, and fell upon her with such impetuosity that the young lady lost her innocence without, so to speak, realizing that she had done so. And when, having recovered from her surprise, she exclaimed: "Is it you, Seigneur Maxime? What are you doing here?" and was preparing as in duty bound to resist her aggressor, he was quietly walking down the street, readjusting his armour and ogling the girls.

Possibly she would have entirely overlooked this offence, had it not been that some time later she found that she was about to become a mother. Captain Maxime was then fighting in Mambournia. All the town knew her shame: she confided it to the great St. Nicolas, who, on learning this astonishing news, lifted his eyes to heaven, and said:

"Lord, did you rescue this man from the salting-tub only as a ravening wolf to devour my sheep? Your wisdom is adorable; but your ways are dark, and your designs mysterious."

And in that same year, on the Sunday of Mid-Lent, Sulpice threw himself at the feet of the holy Bishop, saying:

"From my earliest youth, my keenest wish has been to consecrate myself to the Lord. Allow me, father, to embrace the monastic state, and to make my profession in the monastery of the mendicant friars of Trinqueballe."

"My son," answered the good St. Nicolas, "there is no worthier condition than that of the monk. Happy is he who in the shade of the cloister takes shelter from the tempests of the age. But of what avail to flee the storm if the storm is within oneself? Of what avail to affect an outward show of humility, if one's bosom contains a heart full of pride? What shall you profit by donning the livery of obedience if your soul be in revolt? I have seen you, my son, fall into more errors than Sabellius, Arius, Nestorius, Eutyches, Manes, Pelagius, and Pachosius combined, and revive, before your twentieth year, twelve centuries of peculiar opinions. It is true that you have not been very obstinate in any of them, but your successive recantations appear to betray less submission to our Holy Mother the Church than eagerness to rush from one error to another, to leap from Manicheeism to Sabellianism, and from the crime of the Albigenses to the ignominies of the Vaudois."

Sulpice listened to this discourse with a contrite heart, a simplicity of mind and submissiveness, that drew tears from the great St. Nicolas.

"I deplore, repudiate, condemn, reprove, detest, execrate, and abominate my errors, past, present, and future," he said. "I submit myself to the

Church fully and entirely, totally and generally, purely and simply; and I have no belief but her belief, no faith but her faith, no knowledge but her knowledge: I neither see, hear, nor feel, save only through her. She might tell me that the fly which has but now settled on the nose of the Deacon Modernus was a camel, and I should incontinently, without dispute, contest, murmur, resistance, hesitation or doubt, believe, declare, proclaim, and confess, under torture and unto death, that it was a camel that settled on the nose of the Deacon Modernus. For the Church is the Fountain of Truth, and I am nought by myself but a vile receptacle of Error."

"Take care, my father," said Modernus. "Sulpice is capable of overdoing submission to the Church even to the point of Heresy. Do you not see that he submits with frenzy, in transports and swooning? Is wallowing in submission a good way of submitting? He is annihilating himself; he is committing suicide."

But the Bishop reprimanded his deacon for holding such ideas, which were contrary to charity, and sent the postulant to the noviciate of the mendicant friars of Trinqueballe.

Alas, at the end of a year those priests, till then so quiet and humble, were torn by frightful schisms, plunged into a thousand errors against the Catholic truth, their days filled with disorder, and their souls with sedition! Sulpice inspired the brothers with this poison. He sustained against his superiors that there was no longer any true Pope, since miracles no longer accompanied the elections of the Sovereign Pontiffs; nor, rightly speaking, any Church, since Christians had ceased to live the life of the apostles and the first of the faithful; that there was no purgatory; that it was not necessary to confess to a priest if one confessed to God; that men do wrong in making use of moneys of gold and silver, for they should share in common the fruits of the earth. These abominable maxims, which he forcibly sustained, were combated by some, and adopted by others, causing horrible scandals. A little later Sulpice taught the doctrine of perfect purity, which nothing can soil, and the good brothers' monastery became like a cage of monkeys. This pestilence did not remain confined within the walls of a monastery. Sulpice went preaching through the city; his eloquence, the internal fire by which he was consumed, the simplicity of his life, and his unshakable courage touched all hearts.

On hearing the voice of the reformer, the ancient city, evangelized by St. Cromadaire, and enlightened by St. Gibbosine, fell into disorder and dissolution; every sort of extravagance and impiety was committed there, by day and by night. In vain did the great St. Nicolas warn his flock by exhortations, threats, and fulminations. The evil increased unchecked, and it was sad to see the contagion spreading itself among the well-to-do townsfolk, the lords, and the clergy, as much as and more than among the poor artisans and the small tradesfolk.

One day when the man of God was lamenting the deplorable state of the church of Vervignole in the cloister of the cathedral, his meditations were disturbed by strange shrieks, and he saw a woman, stark naked, walking on all fours, with a peacock's feather for a tail. As she came nearer, she barked, sniffed, and licked the ground. Her fair head was covered with mud, and her whole body was a mass of filth. In this unhappy creature the holy Bishop Nicolas recognized his niece Mirande.

"What do you there, my daughter?" he cried. "Why are you naked, and wherefore do you walk on your hands and knees? Have you no shame?"

"No, uncle, I am not ashamed," sweetly replied Mirande. "I should, on the contrary, be ashamed of any other gesture, or method of progression. If one wishes to please God, it is thus that one should behave. The holy Brother Sulpice taught me to conduct myself thus, in order to resemble the beasts, who are nearer to God than is Man, in that they have not sinned. So long as I am in the state in which you see me, there will be no danger of my sinning. I have come, uncle, to beg you in all love and charity to do likewise; for unless you do you cannot be saved. Remove, I beg, your clothes, and adopt the posture of the animals, in whom God joyfully sees His image which has not been distorted by sin. I give you this advice by order of the holy brother Sulpice, and consequently by order of God Himself, for the holy brother is in the Lord's secrets. Strip yourself naked, uncle, and come with me, so that we may show ourselves to the people for their edification."

"Can I believe my eyes and ears?" gasped the holy Bishop, whose voice was stifled by sobs. "I had a niece blooming in beauty, virtue, and piety; the three children whom I rescued from the salting-tub have reduced her to the miserable condition in which I now see her. The first has despoiled her of all her property, an abundant source of alms, and the patrimony of the poor; the second has robbed her of her honour, and the third has turned her into a heretic."

He threw himself on the flagstones, embracing his niece, begging her to renounce so evil a way of life, and adjuring her to reclothe herself, and walk on her feet like a human being, ransomed by the blood of Jesus Christ.

But she replied only by sharp yelps and lamentable shrieks.

Before long the town of Trinqueballe was filled with naked men and women, walking on all fours and barking; they called themselves the Edenites, and their ambition was to lead back the world to the times of perfect innocence, before the unfortunate creation of Adam and Eve.

The Reverend Father Gilles Caquerole, a Dominican, inquisitor of the faith in the city, university, and ecclesiastical province of Trinqueballe, became uneasy concerning this novelty, and proceeded to look into it minutely. In the most urgent fashion, by letters under his seal, he invited the Bishop Nicolas, in co-operation with himself, to arrest, imprison, interrogate, and sentence these enemies of God, and especially their principal leaders, the Franciscan monk, Sulpice, and a dissolute woman named Mirande. The great St. Nicolas burned with an ardent zeal for the unity of the Church and the destruction of heresy, but he dearly loved his niece. He hid her in the episcopal palace, and refused to hand her over to the inquisitor Caquerole, who denounced him to the Pope as an abettor of disorder and the propagator of a new and very detestable heresy. The Pope enjoined Nicolas to no longer withhold the guilty one from her legitimate judges. Nicolas eluded the injunction, protested his obedience, and did not obey. The Pope fulminated against him in the Bull *Maleficus pastor*, in which the venerable pontiff was accused of being a disobedient member of the Church, a heretic, or one smelling of heresy, a keeper of concubines, a committer of incest, a corrupter of the people, an old woman and a meddling old fool, and was passionately admonished.

In this way the Bishop did himself a great deal of harm without any benefit to his beloved niece. King Berlu, having been threatened with excommunication if he did not lend his secular arm to the Church in pursuit of the Edenites, sent some men-at-arms to the episcopal palace of Trinqueballe. They tore Mirande from her asylum: she was brought before the inquisitor Caquerole, thrown into a deep dungeon, and fed upon bread which the jailers' dogs had refused; but what afflicted her most was that she was forcibly compelled to don an old frock and a hood, and that she could no longer be certain of not sinning.

The monk Sulpice escaped the investigations of the Holy Office and succeeded in reaching Mambournia, and found an asylum in a monastery of that kingdom, where he established new sects even more pernicious than the previous one.

Nevertheless, heresy, fortified by persecution, and exulting in danger, now spread its ravages over the whole of Vervignole. All over the kingdom there were seen in the fields thousands of naked men and women, nibbling the grass, bleating, lowing, roaring, neighing, and contending at night with sheep, cattle, and horses for the use of stable and manger. The inquisitor informed the Holy Father of these horrible scandals, and warned him that so long as the Protector of the Edenites, the odious Nicolas, remained seated on the throne of St. Cromadaire, the evil could only continue to increase. Conformably with this advice the Pope hurled against the Bishop, like a thunderbolt, the Bull *Deterrima quondam*, by which he deprived him of all his ecclesiastical functions, and cut him off from the communion of the faithful.

CHAPTER VI

CRUSHED by the Vicar of Jesus Christ, steeped in bitterness, overwhelmed by affliction, the holy Nicolas stepped down without regret from his illustrious seat, and departed, no more to return thither, from the city of Trinqueballe, which for thirty years had witnessed his pontifical virtues and apostolic labours. There is in western Vervignole a lofty mountain, whose peaks are covered with perpetual snow; from its flanks there descend, in spring, the foaming sonorous cascades that fill the valley torrents with a water as blue as the sky. There, in a region where grow the larch, the arbutus, and the hazel, some hermits supported themselves on berries and milk. This mountain is called that of the Saviour. It was here that St. Nicolas resolved to take refuge, and, far from the world, to weep for his sins and those of man.

As he was climbing the mountain in search of some wild spot where he might establish his habitation, having emerged above the clouds which are almost always gathered about the flanks of the peak, he saw upon the threshold of a hut an old man sharing his bread with a tame hind. His hair fell over his forehead, and nothing could be perceived of his face but the tip of his nose and a long white beard.

The holy Nicolas greeted him with these words:

"Peace be with you, brother."

"It delights to dwell upon this mountain," answered the recluse.

"I also," replied the holy Nicolas, "have come hither to end, in calm, days which have been disturbed by the tumult of the times and the malignity of men."

As he was speaking in this wise, the hermit gazed at him attentively.

"Are you not," he said at length, "the Bishop of Trinqueballe, that Nicolas whose works and virtues are extolled by men?"

When, by a sign, the holy pontiff admitted that he was that man, the hermit threw himself at his feet.

"Monseigneur, to you I owe the saving of my soul, if, as I hope, my soul is saved."

Nicolas raised him with kindness, and asked him:

"My brother, how have I had the happiness to work for your salvation?"

"Twenty years ago," replied the recluse, "when I was an innkeeper at the edge of a wood, on a deserted road, I saw one day, in a field, three little children gleaning. I lured them to my house, gave them wine to drink, cut their throats in their sleep, cut them up into small pieces, and salted them. On seeing them emerge from the salting-tub I was frozen with terror; owing to your exhortations my heart melted; I experienced a salutary repentance, and, fleeing from men, I came to this mountain, where I consecrated my days to God. He bestowed His peace upon me."

"What," cried the holy Bishop, "you are that cruel Garum, guilty of so heinous a crime! I praise God that he has accorded you a peaceful heart, after the horrible murder of three children, whom you put in the salting-tub like pigs; but as for me, alas! for having drawn them out of it my life has been filled with tribulation, my soul steeped in bitterness, and my Bishopric laid wholly desolate. I have been deposed, excommunicated by the common Father of the Faithful. Why have I been so cruelly punished for what I did?"

"Let us worship God," said Garum, "and let us not ask His motives."

The great St. Nicolas, with his own hands, built a hut near that of Garum, and there, in prayer and penitence, he ended his days.

THE STORY OF THE DUCHESS OF CICOGNE AND OF MONSIEUR DE BOULINGRIN

THE STORY OF THE DUCHESS OF CICOGNE AND OF MONSIEUR DE BOULINGRIN

CHAPTER I

THE story of the Sleeping Beauty is well known; we have excellent accounts of it, both in prose and in verse. I shall not undertake to relate it again; but, having become acquainted with several memoirs of the time which have remained unpublished, I discovered some anecdotes relating to King Cloche and Queen Satine, whose daughter it was that slept a hundred years, and also to several members of the Court who shared the Princess's sleep. I propose to communicate to the public such portions of these revelations as have seemed to me most interesting.

After several years of marriage, Queen Satine gave the King, her husband, a daughter who received the names of Paule-Marie-Aurore. The baptismal festivities were planned by the Duc des Hoisons, grand master of the ceremonies, in accordance with a formulary dating from the Emperor Honorius, which was so mildewed and so nibbled by rats that it was impossible to decipher any of it.

There were still fairies in those days, and those who had titles used to go to Court. Seven of them were invited to be god-mothers, Queen Titania, Queen Mab, the wise Vivien, trained by Merlin in the arts of enchantment, Melusina, whose history was written by Jean d'Arras, and who became a serpent every Saturday (but the baptism was on a Sunday), Urgèle, White Anna of Brittany, and Mourgue who led Ogier the Dane into the country of Avalon.

They appeared at the castle in robes of the colour of time, of the sun, of the moon, and of the nymphs, all glittering with diamonds and pearls. As all were taking their places at table an old fairy called Alcuine, who had not been invited, was seen to enter.

"Pray do not be annoyed, madame," said the King, "that you were not of those invited to this festivity; it was believed that you were either dead or enchanted."

Since the fairies grew old, there is no doubt that they used to die. They all died in time, and everybody knows that Melusina became a kitchen wench in Hell. By means of enchantment they could be imprisoned in a magic circle, a tree, a bush, or a stone, or changed into a statue, a hind, a dove, a footstool, a ring, or a slipper. But as a fact it was not because they thought her dead or enchanted that they had not invited the fairy Alcuine; it was because her presence at the banquet had been regarded as contrary to etiquette. Madame de Maintenon was able to state without the least exaggeration that "there are no austerities in the convents like those to which Court etiquette subjects the great." In accordance with his sovereign's royal wish the Duc des Hoisons had not invited the fairy Alcuine, because she had one quartering of nobility too few to be admitted to Court. When the Ministers of State represented that it was of the utmost importance to humour this powerful and vindictive fairy, of whom they would make a dangerous enemy if they excluded her from the festivities, the King replied in peremptory tones that she could not be invited, as she was not qualified by birth.

This unhappy monarch, even more than his predecessors, was a slave to etiquette. His obstinacy in subordinating the greatest interests and most urgent duties to the smallest exigencies of an obsolete ceremonial, had more than once caused serious loss to the monarchy, and had involved the realm in formidable perils. Of all these perils and losses, those to which Cloche had exposed his house by refusing to stretch a point of etiquette in favour of a fairy, without birth, yet formidable and illustrious, were by no means the hardest to foresee, nor was it least urgent to avert them.

The aged Alcuine, enraged by the contempt to which she had been subjected, bestowed upon the Princess Aurore a disastrous gift. At fifteen years of age, beautiful as the day, this royal child was to die of a fatal wound, caused by a spindle, an innocent weapon in the hands of mortal women, but a terrible one when the three spinstress Sisters twist and coil thereon the thread of our destinies and the strings of our hearts.

The seven godmothers could modify, but could not annul Alcuine's decree, and thus the fate of the Princess was determined. "Aurore will prick her hand with a spindle; she will not die of it, but will fall into a sleep of a hundred years, from which the son of a king will come to arouse her."

CHAPTER II

ANXIOUSLY the King and Queen consulted, in respect of the decree pronounced upon the Princess in her cradle, all persons of learning and judgment, notably Monsieur Gerberoy, perpetual secretary of the Academy of Sciences, and Dr. Gastinel, the Queen's accoucheur.

"Monsieur Gerberoy," Satine inquired, "can one really sleep a hundred years?"

"Madame," answered the Academician, "we have examples of sleep, more or less prolonged, some of which I can relate to Your Majesty. Epimenides of Cnossos was born of the loves of a mortal and a nymph. While yet a child he was sent by Dosiades, his father, to watch the flocks in the mountains. When the warmth of midday enveloped the earth, he laid himself down in a cool, dark cave, and there he fell into a slumber which lasted for fifty-seven years. He studied the virtues of the plants, and died, according to some, at the age of a hundred and fifty-four years; according to others at the age of two hundred and ninety-eight.

"The story of the seven sleepers of Ephesus is

related by Theodore and Rufinus, in a manuscript sealed with two silver seals. Briefly expounded, these are the principal facts. In the year 25 of our Lord, seven of the officers of the Emperor Decius, who had embraced the Christian religion, distributed their goods to the poor, retired to Mount Celion, and there all seven fell asleep in a cave. During the reign of Theodore the Bishop of Ephesus found them there, blooming like roses. They had slept for one hundred and forty-four years.

"Frederick Barbarossa is still asleep. In the crypt beneath a ruined castle, in the midst of a dense forest, he is seated before a table round which his beard has twisted seven times. He will awake to drive away the crows which croak around the mountain.

"These, madame, are the greatest sleepers of whom History has kept a record."

"They are all exceptions," answered the Queen. "You, Monsieur Gastinel, who practise medicine, have you ever seen people sleep a hundred years?"

"No, madame," replied the accoucheur, "I have not exactly seen any such, nor do I ever expect to do so; but I have seen some curious cases of lethargy, which, if you desire, I will bring to Your Majesty's notice.

"Ten years ago a demoiselle Jeanne Caillou, being admitted to the Hôtel-Dieu, there slept for six consecutive years. I myself observed the girl Léonide Montauciel, who fell asleep on Easter Day in the year '61, and did not awake until Easter Day of the following year."

"Monsieur Gastinel," demanded the King, "can the point of a spindle cause a wound which will send one to sleep for a hundred years?"

"Sire, it is not probable," answered Monsieur Gastinel, "but in the domain of pathology, we can never say with certainty, 'This will or will not happen.'"

"One might mention Brunhild," said Monsieur Gerberoy, "who was pricked by a thorn, fell asleep, and was awakened by Sigurd."

"There was also Guenillon," said the Duchess of Cicogne, first lady-in-waiting to the Queen. And she hummed:

She was sent to the wood
To gather some nuts,
The bush was too high,
The maid was too small.

The bush was too high,
The maid was too small,
She pricked her poor hand
With a very sharp thorn.

She pricked her poor hand
With a very sharp thorn,
From the pain in her finger
The maid fell asleep.

"What are you thinking of, Cicogne?" said the Queen. "You are singing."

"Your Majesty will forgive me," replied the Duchess. "It was to ward off the bad luck."

The King issued an edict, whereby all persons were forbidden under pain of death to spin with spindles, or even to have spindles in their possession. All obeyed. They still used to say in the country districts: "The spindles must follow the mattock," but it was only by force of habit. The spindles had disappeared.

CHAPTER III

ONSIEUR DE LA ROCHECOUPÉE, the Prime Minister who, under the feeble King Cloche, governed the kingdom, respected popular beliefs, as all great statesmen respect them. Cæsar was Pontifex Maximus, and Napoleon had himself crowned by the Pope. Monsieur de La Rochecoupée admitted the power of the fairies. He was by no means sceptical, by no means incredulous. He did not suggest that the prediction of the seven godmothers was false. But, being helpless, he did not allow it to disturb him. His temperament was such that he did not worry about evils which he was impotent to remedy. In any case, so far as could be judged, the occurrence foretold was not imminent. Monsieur de La Rochecoupée viewed events as a statesman, and statesmen never look beyond the present moment. I am speaking of the shrewdest and most far-sighted. After all, supposing one day the King's daughter did fall asleep for a hundred years, it was, in his eyes, purely a family matter, seeing that women were excluded from the throne by the Salic Law.

He had, as he said, plenty of other fish to fry. Bankruptcy, hideous bankruptcy was ever present, threatening to consume the wealth and the honour of the nation. Famine was raging in the kingdom, and millions of unfortunate wretches were eating plaster instead of bread. That year the opera ball was more brilliant and the masques finer than ever.

The peasantry, artisans, and shopkeepers, and the girls of the theatre, vied with one another in grieving over the fatal curse inflicted by Alcuine upon the innocent Princess. The lords of the Court, on the contrary, and the princes of the blood royal, appeared very indifferent to it. And there were on all hands men of business and students of science who did not believe in the award of the fairies, for the very good reason that they did not believe in fairies.

Such a one was Monsieur Boulingrin, Secretary of State for the Treasury. Those who ask how it was possible that he should not believe in them since he had seen them are unaware of the lengths to which scepticism can go in an argumentative mind. Nourished on Lucretius, imbued with the doctrines of Epicurus and Gassendi, he often provoked

Monsieur de La Rochecoupée by the display of a cold disbelief in fairies.

The Prime Minister would say to him: "If not for your own sake, be a believer for that of the public. Seriously, my dear Boulingrin, that there are moments when I wonder which of us two is the more credulous in respect of fairies. I never think of them, and you are always talking of them."

Monsieur de Boulingrin dearly loved the Duchess of Cicogne, wife of the ambassador to Vienna, first lady-in-waiting to the Queen, who belonged to the highest aristocracy of the realm; a witty woman, somewhat lean, and a trifle close, who was losing her income, her estates, and her very chemise at faro. She showed much kindness to Monsieur de Boulingrin, lending herself to an intercourse for which she had no temperamental inclination, but which she thought suitable to her rank, and useful to her interests. Their intrigue was conducted with an art which revealed their good taste, and the elegance of the prevailing morality; the connection was openly avowed, and thereby stripped of all base hypocrisy; but it was at the same time so reserved in appearance that even the severest critics saw no cause for censure in it.

During the time which the Duchess yearly spent on her estate, Monsieur de Boulingrin used to stay in an old pigeon-house, separated from his friend's château by a sunken road, which skirted a marsh, where by night the frogs among the reeds tuned their diligent voices.

Now, one evening when the last rays of the setting sun were dying the stagnant water with the hue of blood, the Secretary of State for the Treasury saw at the cross-roads three young fairies who were dancing in a circle and singing :

> " Trois filles dedans un pré
> Mon cœur vole
> Mon cœur vole
> Mon cœur vole à votre gré."

They enclosed him within their circle, and their light and airy forms sped swiftly about him. Their faces, in the twilight, were dim and transparent ; their tresses shone like the will-o'-the-wisp.

They repeated :

> " Trois filles dedans un pré ! "

until, dazed and ready to fall, he begged for mercy.

Then said the most beautiful, opening the circle :

" Sisters, give leave to Monsieur de Boulingrin to pass, that he may go to the castle, and kiss his lady-love."

He went on without having recognized the fairies, the mistresses of men's destinies, and a little farther on he met three old beggar women, who were walking bowed low over their sticks; their faces were like three apples roasted in the cinders. From their rags protruded bones which had more dirt than flesh upon them. Their naked feet ended in fleshless toes of immoderate length, like the bones of an ox-tail.

As soon as they saw him approaching they smiled upon him and threw him kisses; they stopped him on his way, calling him their darling, their love, their pet, and covered him with caresses which he was powerless to evade, for the moment he made a movement to escape, they dug into his flesh the sharp claws at the tips of their fingers.

"Isn't he handsome? Isn't he lovely?" they sighed.

For some time they raved on, begging him to love them. Then, seeing they could not rouse his senses, which were frozen with horror, they covered him with abuse, hammered him with their staves, threw him on the ground and trod him underfoot. Then, when he was crushed, broken, aching, and crippled in every limb, the youngest, who was at least eighty years of age, squatted upon him and treated him in a manner too infamous to describe. He was almost suffocated; immediately afterwards the other two, taking the place of the first, treated the unfortunate gentleman in the same way.

Finally all three made off, saluting him with: "Good night, Endymion!" "To our next meeting, Adonis!" "Good-bye, beautiful Narcissus!" and left him swooning.

When he came back to his senses, a toad near him was whistling deliciously like a flute, and a cloud of mosquitoes were dancing before the moon. He rose with great difficulty and limpingly pursued his journey.

Once again Monsieur de Boulingrin had failed to recognize the fairies, mistresses of the destinies of men.

The Duchess of Cicogne awaited him impatiently.

"You come very late, my friend," she said.

He answered, as he kissed her fingers, that it was very kind of her to reproach him. His excuse was that he had been somewhat unwell.

"Boulingrin," she said, "sit down there."

And she confided to him that she would be very happy to accept from the royal treasury a present of two thousand crowns, as a fitting compensation for the unkindness of fate, faro having for the last six months been terribly against her.

Informed that the matter was urgent, Boulingrin wrote immediately to Monsieur de La Rochecoupée to ask for the necessary sum of money.

"La Rochecoupée will be delighted to obtain it for you," he said. "He is a helpful person and takes pleasure in serving his friends. I may add that in him one perceives greater talents than are commonly seen in the favourites of Princes. He has taste, and a head for business ; but he is lacking in philosophy. He believes in fairies, relying on his senses——"

"Boulingrin," said the Duchess, "you stink like a tom-cat."

CHAPTER IV

SEVENTEEN years, day by day, had elapsed since the fairies' decree. The Princess was as beautiful as a star. The King, Queen, and Court were in residence at the rural palace of Eaux-Perdues. Need I relate what happened then? It is well known how the Princess Aurore, wandering one day through the castle, came to the top of a keep, where, in a garret, she found a dear old woman, all alone, plying her distaff. She had never heard of the King's regulations, forbidding the use of spindles.

"What are you doing, my good woman?" asked the Princess.

"I am spinning, my dear child," replied the old woman, who did not recognize her.

"Ah, how pretty it looks," replied the Princess. "How do you do it? Give it to me, that I may see if I can do it as well."

No sooner had she picked up the spindle, than she pricked her hand with it, and fell swooning.[1]

King Cloche, when he heard that the fairies'

[1] *Contes de Perrault*, édition André Lefèvre, p. 86.

decree had been accomplished, ordered that the sleeping Princess should be placed in the Blue Chamber, on a bed of azure embroidered with silver.

Shocked, and full of consternation, the courtiers made ready to weep, practised sighing, and assumed an expression of deep affliction. Intrigues were formed in every direction ; it was reported that the King had discharged his Ministers. The blackest calumnies were hatched. It was said that the Duc de La Rochecoupée had concocted a draught to send the Princess to sleep, and that Monsieur de Boulingrin was his accomplice.

The Duchess of Cicogne climbed the secret staircase to the chambers of her old friend, whom she found in his night-cap, smiling, for he was reading *La Fiancée du roi de Garbe.*

Cicogne told him the news, and how the Princess was lying on a blue bed in a state of lethargy.

The Secretary of State listened attentively.

"You do not believe, I hope, my dear friend, that the fairies have anything to do with it?" he said.

For he did not believe in fairies, although three of them, ancient and venerable, had overpowered him with their love and their staves, and had drenched him to the skin in a disgusting liquid, in order to prove their existence to him. The defect of the experimental method pursued by these ladies is that the experiment was addressed to the senses, whose testimony one can always challenge.

"The fairies have had everything to do with it!" cried the Duchess. "The Princess's accident may have the most unfortunate results for you and for me. People will not fail to attribute it to the incapacity of the Ministers, and possibly to their malevolence. Can one tell how far calumny may reach? You are already accused of niggardliness. According to what is being said, you refused, on my advice, to pay for warders for the young and unfortunate Princess. Worse than that, there are rumours of black magic, of casting spells. The storm has got to be faced. Show yourself, or you are lost!"

"Calumny," said Boulingrin, "is the curse of this world. It has killed the greatest of men. Whoever honestly serves his King must make up his mind to pay tribute to that crawling, flying horror."

"Boulingrin," said Cicogne, "get dressed." And she snatched off his night-cap, and threw it down by the bed-side.

A few minutes later they were in the antechamber of the apartment in which Aurore was sleeping, and seating themselves on a bench they waited to be introduced.

Now at the news that the decree of the Fates had been accomplished, the fairy Vivien, one of the Princess's godmothers, repaired in great haste to Eaux-Perdues, and in order that when she awoke her god-daughter should have a Court she touched every one in the castle with her ring. "Governesses, maids of honour, women of the bedchamber, noblemen, officers, grooms of the chamber, cooks, scullions, messengers, guards, beadles, pages, and footmen ; she also touched the horses in the stables, the grooms, the great mastiffs in the yard, and little Pouffe, the Princess's lap-dog, which lay near her upon her bed. The very spits in front of the fire, loaded with pheasants and partridges, went to sleep."[1]

Meanwhile, Cicogne and Boulingrin waited side by side upon their bench.

"Boulingrin," whispered the Duchess in her old friend's ear, "does it not seem to you that there is something suspicious in this business? Don't you suspect an intrigue on the part of the King's brothers to get the poor man to abdicate? He is well known as a good father. They may well have wished to throw him into despair."

"It is possible," answered the Secretary of State. "In any case the fairies have nothing whatever to do with the matter. Only old countrywomen can still believe these cock-and-bull stories."

[1] *Contes de Perrault*, p. 87.

"Be quiet, Boulingrin," said the Duchess. "There is nothing so hateful as a sceptic. He is an impertinent person who laughs at our simplicity. I detest strong-minded people; I believe what I ought to believe; but in this particular case, I suspect a dark intrigue."

At the moment when Cicogne spoke these words, the fairy Vivien touched them both with her ring, and sent them to sleep like the rest.

CHAPTER V

"IN a quarter of an hour there grew all round about the park such an immense quantity of trees, large and small, with thorns and briars interlaced, that neither man nor beast could pass; so that only the tops of the castle towers could be seen, and these only from a long way off."[1]

Once, twice, thrice, fifty, sixty, eighty, ninety, and a hundred times did Urania close the circle of Time: the Sleeping Beauty and her Court, with Boulingrin beside the Duchess on the bench in the antechamber, still slept on.

Whether one regard Time as a mode of the unique substance, whether it be defined as one of the forms of the conscious ego, or an abstract phase of the immediate externality, or whether one regard it purely as a law, a relation resulting from the progression of Reality, we can affirm that one hundred years is a certain space of time.

[1] *Contes de Perrault*, pp. 87–88.

CHAPTER VI

EVERY one knows the end of the enchantment, and how, after a hundred terrestrial cycles, a prince favoured by the fairies penetrated the enchanted wood, and reached the bed where slept the Princess. He was a little German princeling, with a pretty moustache, and rounded hips. As soon as she woke up, she fell, or rather rose so much in love, that she followed him to his little principality in such a hurry that she never said a word to the people of her household, who had slept with her for a hundred years.

Her first lady-in-waiting was quite touched thereby, and exclaimed with admiration :

" I recognize the blood of my kings."

Boulingrin woke up beside the Duchess de Cicogne at the same time as the Princess and all her household.

As he rubbed his eyes, his mistress said :

" Boulingrin, you have been asleep."

" Not at all, dear lady, not at all."

He spoke in good faith. Having slept without

dreaming for a hundred years, he did not know that he had been asleep.

"I have been so little asleep," he said, "that I can repeat what you said a minute ago."

"Well, what did I say?"

"You said, 'I suspect a dark intrigue.'"

As soon as it awoke, the whole of the little Court was discharged; every one had to fend for himself as best he could.

Boulingrin and Cicogne hired from the castle steward an old seventeenth-century trap drawn by an animal which was already very aged before it went to sleep for a hundred years, and drove to the station of Eaux-Perdues, where they caught a train which, in two hours, deposited them in the capital of the country. Great was their surprise at all that they saw and heard. But by the end of a quarter of an hour they had exhausted their astonishment, and nothing surprised them any more. As for themselves, nobody took the slightest interest in them. Their story was perfectly incomprehensible, and awakened no curiosity, for our minds are not interested in anything that is too obvious, or too difficult to follow.

As one may well believe, Boulingrin had not the remotest idea what had happened to him. But when the Duchess said that it was not natural, he answered:

"Dear lady, allow me to observe that you have been badly trained in physics. Nothing exists which is not according to Nature."

There remained to them neither friends, relations, nor property. They could not identify the position of their house. With the little money they had they bought a guitar, and sang in the streets. By this means they gained sufficient to support themselves. At night Cicogne staked at manille, in the inns, the coppers that had been thrown her during the day, while Boulingrin, with a bowl of warm wine in front of him, explained to the company that it was ridiculous to believe in fairies.

THE SHIRT

"It was only a young shepherd, listlessly reclining upon the grass of the meadow, and beguiling his solitude by the notes of a pipe. His clothes had been forcibly removed, but . . ." (*Grand Dictionnaire*, de Pierre Larousse, article "Chemise," t. IV, p. 5, col. 4).

THE SHIRT

CHAPTER I

KING CHRISTOPHE, HIS GOVERNMENT, HIS HABITS AND HIS MALADY

CHRISTOPHE V was not a bad king. He minutely observed the rules of Parliamentary government, and he never opposed the will of the Chambers. This submission did not cost him very much, for he had observed that while there are several means of attaining power, there is only one means of retaining it, and only one way of behaving when it is yours; that whatever were the origin, principles, ideas, and opinions of his ministers, they all governed in one and the same fashion; and that, despite certain purely formal divergencies, they repeated one another's sayings with reassuring exactitude. Unhesitatingly, therefore, he appointed to power all those persons nominated by the Chambers, always preferring the revolutionaries, as being the most eager to impose their authority.

For his own part, he applied himself more

especially to foreign affairs. He frequently made diplomatic journeys, dined and hunted with the kings, his cousins, and boasted himself to be the best Foreign Minister imaginable. When at home he kept himself in countenance as well as the miseries of the times would allow. He was neither greatly loved nor greatly respected by his people, which assured him of this inestimable advantage, that he could never cause disappointment. Exempt from the affections of the public, he was never threatened by the unpopularity which is the assured lot of whomsoever is popular.

His kingdom was wealthy. Commerce and industry flourished there, yet without undergoing such expansion as to cause anxiety to neighbouring States. Above all, its finances commanded admiration. The solidity of its credit appeared unshakable; financiers referred to it with enthusiasm and affection, their eyes moist with generous tears And thereby a certain honour was reflected upon King Christophe.

The peasants held him responsible for the bad harvests, but these were rare. The fertility of the soil and the patience of the tillers caused the land to abound in fruits and grains, wines and flocks. The factory hands, by their violent and unceasing demands, alarmed the middles classes, who relied on the King to protect them from the social revolution: the workers, on the other hand, could not overthrow him, for they were the weaker; nor did they wish to do so, since they could not see that they had anything to gain by his fall. He never assisted them, neither did he oppress them, with the result that they were always a menace and never a danger.

The sovereign could count upon the army; its tone was good. The tone of the army invariably is good; all measures are taken to ensure that it shall remain so; this is the first necessity of the State. For were it to lose this tone the Government would be overthrown immediately.

King Christophe protected religion. Truth to tell, he was not a devout person, and in order that his ideas should not be contrary to his faith, he took the useful precaution of never examining a single article of the latter. He heard Mass in his chapel, and was always pressing respectful attentions and favours upon his bishops, amongst whom were to be found three or four ultramontanes who overwhelmed him with abuse.

The baseness and servility of his magistracy inspired him with an insurmountable disgust. He could not conceive how his subjects could endure so unjust a justice; but these magistrates counterbalanced their shameful weakness in respect of the strong by an inflexible harshness toward the weak.

Their severity reassured " the interests " and commanded respect.

Christophe V had noticed that his decrees produced either no appreciable effect whatever, or else results which were the contrary of those which he expected. Consequently he refrained from action. His orders and decorations were his best instruments of sovereignty. He awarded them to his opponents, who were thereby degraded and satisfied.

The Queen had presented him with three sons. She was ugly, shrewish, stupid, and avaricious, but the people, who knew that she was neglected and deceived by the King, covered her with praise and homage. After having had experience of a multitude of women of every condition, the King chiefly frequented the society of Madame de la Poule, his intercourse with whom had become a habit. He had always loved novelty in women ; but a strange woman was, for him, no longer a novelty, and the monotony of continual change oppressed him. He would return in disgust to Madame de la Poule, and this lack of novelty which seemed so tedious in those whom he saw for the first time, he bore with more patiently in an old friend. Nevertheless she bored him intensely and persistently. At times, being quite worn out by the insipidity of her eternal sameness, he tried to vary her by disguises, making her dress up as a Tyrolean, an Andalusian, a Capuchin friar, a captain of Dragoons, or a nun; but never for a moment did he fail to find her insipid.

His chief occupation was hunting—an hereditary function of kings and princes, handed down to them from the earliest of mankind; an antique necessity which has become a sport; a toil in which the great find pleasure. There is no pleasure without fatigue. Christophe V hunted six days a week.

One day, in the forest, he said to Monsieur de Quatrefeuilles, his first Equerry:

"What a bore stag-hunting is!"

"Sire," answered the Equerry, "you will be very glad of a rest after the hunt."

"Quatrefeuilles," sighed the King, "there was a time when I took pleasure in getting tired, and then in resting. Now I find no pleasure in either. For me, every occupation has the emptiness of idleness, and rest wearies me as much as painful toil."

After reigning for ten years without wars or revolutions, regarded by his subjects as a clever politician, established as an arbiter by kings, there existed in the world no pleasure for Christophe V to taste. Plunged into the deepest despondency, he would often say:

"I have always black spots before my eyes, and

under the cartilages of my ribs I feel a rock upon which Melancholy is enthroned."

He lost sleep and appetite.

"I can no longer eat," he would say to Monsieur de Quatrefeuilles, seated before his splendid service of silver gilt. "Alas, it is not the pleasures of the table I regret; I never enjoyed them; that is a pleasure no king ever enjoyed. I have the worst table in my kingdom. Only the common folk eat well: the rich have cooks who rob and poison them. The greatest cooks are those that rob and poison the most, and I have the greatest cooks in Europe. All the same, I was naturally greedy, and, like anyone else, I should have loved dainty tit-bits, had my state allowed of it."

He complained of pains in the loins, and weights on his stomach; of weakness, with shortness of breath and palpitation of the heart. Now and again a dull flush of nerveless heat would rise to his face.

"I feel," he used to say, "a still, dull, continuous pain, to which one gets accustomed, which is pierced, from time to time, by sudden flashes of overwhelming agony. Hence my sluggishness and my distress."

His head swam: he suffered from fits of dizziness, headaches, cramps, spasms, and shooting pains in his sides, which stopped his breathing.

The King's two principal physicians, Dr. Saumon and Professor Machellier, diagnosed neurasthenia.

"A morbid unity badly relaxed," said Saumon. "A nosological entity insufficiently defined, and by that very fact indiscernible."

Professor Machellier interrupted him:

"Call it rather, Saumon, a true pathological Proteus, which, like the Old Man of the Sea, incessantly changes its form in the grasp of the practitioner, and assumes the most fantastic and most terrifying shapes; by turns the vulture of the gastric ulcer, or the serpent of nephritis, it suddenly lifts the yellow face of jaundice, displays the red cheek-bones of tuberculosis, or grips with the strangling hands which lead one to believe that there is a hypertrophy of the heart; in short, it represents the spectre of all the disastrous ills that flesh is heir to, until, yielding to medical treatment, and acknowledging itself defeated, it flees in its true shape of simulated disease."

Dr. Saumon was handsome, suave, and charming. He was loved by the ladies, in whom he loved himself. An elegant scientist, a fashionable physician, he could recognize aristocracy even in a cæcum or a peritoneum, and was able exactly to observe the social grades dividing uterus from uterus. Professor Machellier, little, short and fat, shaped like a tub, a profuse talker, was even more foolish than his colleague Saumon. He had the same pretensions, and more difficulty in sustaining them. They loathed each other; but, having perceived that by quarrelling they would mutually destroy one another, they affected a perfect understanding, and a complete communion of thought: no sooner had one expressed an idea than the other made it his. Although each had a hearty contempt for the other's ability and intelligence, they feared not to exchange opinions between themselves, knowing that they risked nothing, neither losing nor gaining by the exchange, seeing they were merely medical opinions.

At first the King's illness caused them no uneasiness. They hoped that the patient would recover while they were treating him, and that this coincidence would be noted to their advantage. With common accord they prescribed an austere life (*Quibus nervi dolent Venus inimica*), a tonic diet, exercise in the open air, and a carefully considered application of hydrotherapy. Saumon, with the approval of Machellier, prescribed sulphuret of carbon and methyl-chloride; Machellier, Saumon acquiescing, indicated opiates, chloral and bromides.

But several months elapsed, and the King's condition did not seem to improve in the least. And presently his sufferings became more acute.

"I feel," said Christophe V to them one day,

lying on a long chair, " as if a nest of rats were nibbling my bowels, whilst a horrible dwarf, a hooded goblin, wearing a red tunic, and shoes, had gone down into my stomach, and was attacking it with a pickaxe, and making a deep hole."

" Sire," said Dr. Saumon, " that is a sympathetic pain."

" I find it antipathetic," answered the King.

Professor Machellier intervened :

" Sire, neither Your Majesty's stomach nor intestine is diseased. If they cause you pain it is, we will say, in sympathy with your solar plexus, whose innumerable nervous fibres, mingled and confused, tug in all directions at the bowel and the stomach like so many incandescent platinum wires."

" Neurasthenia," said Machellier, " a true pathological Proteus."

But the King dismissed them both.

When they had gone :

Monsieur de Saint-Sylvain, the senior private secretary, said :

" Sire, pray consult Dr. Rodrigue."

" Yes, Sire," said Monsieur de Quatrefeuilles, " send for Dr. Rodrigue. There's nothing else to be done."

At that time Dr. Rodrigue was astonishing the world. He was to be seen almost simultaneously in all the countries of the globe. He charged such enormous fees that millionaries recognized his value. His colleagues, all over the world, whatever they thought of his knowledge and character, spoke with respect of a man who had raised medical fees to a figure hitherto unheard of. Many praised his methods, pretending that they had mastered them and were applying them at reduced rates, thereby contributing to his world-wide celebrity. But as Dr. Rodrigue was pleased to exclude from his therapeutic all laboratory products and pharmaceutical preparations, and as he never observed the formulæ of the pharmacopeia, his curative methods presented a disconcerting eccentricity and certain inimitable peculiarities.

Monsieur de Saint-Sylvain, although without personal experience of Rodrigue, possessed absolute faith in him, and believed in him as in God.

He begged the King to summon the doctor who worked miracles. In vain.

"I shall stick to Saumon and Machellier," said Christophe V. "I know them, and I know they can do nothing; while I do not know what this Rodrigue might do."

CHAPTER II

DR. RODRIGUE

THE King had never much liked his two usual physicians. After six months' illness he found them perfectly insupportable; as soon as he caught sight of the handsome moustache which crowned Dr. Saumon's everlasting and triumphant smile, and the two wisps of black hair plastered over Machellier's pate, he ground his teeth and savagely averted his glance. One night he threw out of the window all their draughts, pills, and powders, which filled the room with a richly depressing smell. Not only did he cease to carry out their orders, but he even took pains to do the reverse of what they prescribed; he remained lying down when they recommended exercise, moved about when they ordered rest, ate when they put him on diet, fasted when they recommended stuffing; and revealed to Madame de la Poule an ardour so unaccustomed that she was unable to believe the testimony of her senses, and thought she must be dreaming. But he was no whit the better; so true it is that Medicine is a deceptive art, and that its precepts are equally vain in whichever sense one takes them. He got no worse, but he got no better.

His numerous and varied pains never left him. He complained that a colony of ants had established itself in his brain, and that this industrious and warlike community was there digging galleries, chambers, and storehouses, carrying thither provisions and materials; depositing eggs by the thousand, raising young, sustaining sieges, delivering and repulsing assaults, and fighting bloody engagements. He said he could feel it when some warrior cut with his steely mandibles through the hard, thin corselet of an enemy.

"Sire," said Monsieur de Saint-Sylvain, "send for Dr. Rodrigue. He will surely cure you."

But the King shrugged his shoulders, and in a moment of weakness and absent-mindedness he asked once more for medicine, and again began to diet. He no longer visited Madame de la Poule, and zealously swallowed pilules of nitrate of aconitine, which were then in the first flush of their radiant youth. Following on this abstinence and this treatment, he was seized with such an attack of suffocation that his tongue protruded from his mouth and his eyes from his head. His bed was placed standing up like a grandfather's clock, and his congested face looked like a red dial.

"The cardiac plexus is in open rebellion," said Professor Machellier.

"In a state of great effervescence," added Dr. Saumon.

Monsieur de Saint-Sylvain thought it a good opportunity once more to recommend Dr. Rodrigue, but the King declared that he had no need of yet another doctor.

"Sire," answered Saint-Sylvain, "Dr. Rodrigue is not a physician."

"Ah!" exclaimed Christophe V. "What you say, Monsieur de Saint-Sylvain, is all to his advantage, and prejudices me in his favour. If he is not a physician, what is he?"

"A scientist, a man of genius, Sire, who has discovered the marvellous and unsuspected properties of matter in the radiant state, and applies them to medicine."

But the King, in a tone which allowed of no reply, requested his private secretary to refer no more to this charlatan.

"I will never receive him, never!"

Christophe V passed the summer in a fairly tolerable fashion. He went for a cruise in a two-hundred-ton yacht with Madame de la Poule dressed as a cabin-boy. He received at breakfast the President of a Republic, a King and an Emperor, and in conjunction with them assured the peace of the world. It was wearisome work arranging the destinies of the nations, but having found in Madame de la Poule's cabin an old novel of the kind written for shop-girls, he read it with a passionate interest that procured him for some hours a delicious oblivion of reality. In short, except for a few headaches, a few attacks of neuralgia, some touches of rheumatism, and the boredom of existence, he managed fairly well. The autumn brought with it his old tortures. He endured the horrible sufferings of a man wrapped in ice from his waist to his feet, with his chest enveloped in flames. Yet what he suffered with still greater fear and horror were sensations which he was unable to express of unutterable conditions. There were some, he said, which made his hair stand on end. He was eaten up with anæmia, and his weakness increased daily, without diminishing his capacity for suffering.

"Monsieur de Saint-Sylvain," he said one morning, after a bad night, "you have several times spoken to me of Dr. Rodrigue. Send for him."

At that moment Dr. Rodrigue was reported to be at the Cape, in Melbourne, and in St. Petersburg. Cablegrams and radiograms were instantly despatched to these places. Less than a week had passed before the King was urgently asking for Dr. Rodrigue. As the days went by, he asked every minute: "Will he not be here soon?" It was pointed out to him that His Majesty was not a client to be despised, and that Rodrigue was wont to travel with astonishing swiftness. But nothing could calm the sick man's impatience.

"He will not come," he sighed. "You'll see that he will not come."

A telegram arrived from Genoa, announcing that Rodrigue was sailing on board the *Preussen*. Three days later the world-famed doctor, after having paid a visit of insolent deference to his colleagues, Saumon and Machellier, presented himself at the Palace.

He was younger and better looking than Dr. Saumon, with a prouder and more aristocratic air. Out of respect for Nature, whom he obeyed in all things, he allowed his hair and beard to grow, so that he bore a resemblance to those ancient philosophers whom the Greeks have represented in marble.

After examining the King, he said:

"Sire, the physicians, who speak of illnesses as the blind speak of colours, say that you are suffering from neurasthenia, or weakness of the nerves. But, when they have diagnosed your complaint, they will not be any better able to cure it, for an organic tissue cannot be reconstituted save by the same means that Nature employed to build it up, and of these means they are ignorant. Now what are the means, the processes, of Nature? She knows neither hand nor tool; she is subtle and spiritual; for her most powerful and massive constructions she employs the infinitely tenuous particles of matter, the atom, the protyle. From an impalpable mist she makes rocks, metals, plants, animals, and men. How? By attraction, gravitation, transpiration, penetration, imbibition, endosmosis, affinity and sympathy. She makes a grain of sand exactly as she made the Milky Way; the harmony of the spheres reigns equally in both; they both exist by reason of the movement of the particles which compose them, which is their musical soul, amorous and always in motion. Between the stars in the sky, and the dust which is dancing in the ray of sunlight crossing this room, there is no structural difference, and the smallest of these atoms of dust is as wonderful as Sirius, for the miracle in all the bodies of the universe is the infinite minuteness of which they are compact, and by which they are animated. That is how Nature works. From the imperceptible, the impalpable, the imponderable, she has derived this vast world, accessible to our senses, which our mind weighs and measures, and that of which we ourselves are made is no more than a breath. Let us work, as she does, through the imponderable, the impalpable, the imperceptible, by loving attraction and subtle penetration. That is the principle. How shall it be applied in the present case? How to restore life to the exhausted nerves? That is what we have to consider.

"First of all, what are the nerves? If we ask for a definition the meanest physiologist, even a Machellier or a Saumon, will give it us. What are the nerves? They are cords, fibres, which proceed from the brain and the spinal column, and distribute themselves through every part of the body, in order to transmit sensorial excitations, and to cause the motor organs to function. They are therefore sensation and movement. That is enough to teach us their inward constitution, to reveal their essence: by whatever name we call it, it is identical with that which in the order of sensations we call Pleasure, and in the moral order Happiness. Where-ever there is an atom of Pleasure and Happiness there will be found the material that repairs the nerves. When I speak of an atom of Pleasure I refer to a material object, a definite substance, a body capable of passing through the four states, solid, liquid, gaseous and radiant, a body of which one can determine the atomic weight. The joy and sadness of which men, animals, and plants have experienced the effect since the dawn of things are real substances; they are matter, since they are mind, and since under her three aspects of matter, mind, and movement, Nature is one. It is therefore merely a matter of procuring atoms of joy in sufficient numbers, and of introducing them into the system by endosmosis and cutaneous aspiration. For this reason I prescribe that you must wear the shirt of a happy man."

"What!" cried the King. "You wish me to wear the shirt of a happy man?"

"Next your skin, Sire, in order that your dry skin may aspire the particles of Happiness which the sudorific glands of the happy man have exhaled through the excretory canals of his thriving dermis. For you are not ignorant of the functions of the skin; it inspires and exhales, and effects incessant exchanges according to the environment in which it is placed."

"Then that is the remedy which you order me, Monsieur Rodrigue?"

"Sire, it would be impossible to order a more rational one. I find nothing in the pharmacopeia which would takes its place. Ignorant of nature, and incapable of imitating her, our quacks merely concoct a few drugs in their laboratories which are always dangerous and seldom efficacious. The medicaments which we cannot concoct, such as leeches, mountain air, natural thermal waters, asses' milk, wild cat's skin, and the humours exuding from a happy man, we must take ready made. . . .

Do you not know that a raw potato carried in the pocket removes rheumatic pains? You do not want a natural remedy. You prefer artificial or chemical remedies; drugs; you must have drops and powders; but have you much reason to be satisfied with your drops and powders?"

The King apologized, and promised to obey.

Dr. Rodrigue, who had already reached the door, turned and said:

"Let it be slightly warmed before you put it on."

CHAPTER III

MESSIEURS DE QUATREFEUILLES AND DE SAINT-SYLVAIN SEARCH FOR A HAPPY MAN IN THE KING'S PALACE

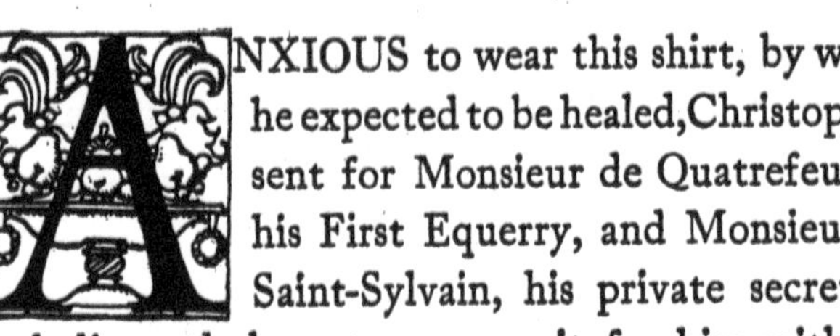

ANXIOUS to wear this shirt, by which he expected to be healed, Christophe V sent for Monsieur de Quatrefeuilles, his First Equerry, and Monsieur de Saint-Sylvain, his private secretary, and directed them to procure it for him with the least possible delay. It was arranged that they should maintain an absolute secrecy with regard to the object of their search. There was indeed reason to fear that if the public came to know the kind of remedy the King required, a host of afflicted persons, and in particular the most unfortunate, the most hopelessly crippled by poverty, would offer their shirts in the hope of a reward. It was also feared that the anarchists might send poisoned shirts.

These two gentlemen considered that they would be able to obtain Dr. Rodrigue's remedy without leaving the Palace, and took up a position in the royal ante-chamber, where they could watch the courtiers go by. Those they saw had a despondent air and emaciated faces; they were consumed with a longing for an appointment, an order, a privilege or a button. But on descending to the great apartments, they found Monsieur du Bocage asleep in an arm-chair. The corners of his mouth turned up to his cheek-bones; his nostrils dilated, his cheeks round and shining like two suns, his throat melodious, his belly quiet and rhythmical; smiling, exuding joy from the top of his glistening cranium down to the turned-out toes of the light slippers which terminated his widely separated legs.

At the sight of him, Quatrefeuilles said:

"We need seek no farther. When he wakes up we will ask him for his shirt."

At that moment the sleeper rubbed his eyes, stretched himself, and looked piteously about him. The corners of his mouth dropped, his cheeks fell, and his eyelids drooped like the washing outside poor folks' windows; his whole person expressed boredom, regret, and disappointment.

Recognizing the equerry and the private secretary, he said:

"Ah, gentlemen, I have just had a beautiful dream. I dreamed that the King had raised my lands of La Bocage to a Marquisate. Alas, it is nothing but a dream, and I know only too well that the King's intentions are quite otherwise."

"Let us get on," said Saint-Sylvain. "It is getting late; we have no time to lose."

In the gallery, they came across a peer of the realm who astonished everybody by the strength of his character, and the profundity of his mind. His enemies did not deny his disinterestedness, his sincerity, or his courage. It was known that he was writing his memoirs, and every one flattered him in the hope that they might cut a respectable figure there in the eyes of posterity.

"Perhaps he is happy," said Saint-Sylvain.

"Let's ask him," said Quatrefeuilles.

They accosted him, exchanged a few remarks, and then, turning the conversation to the subject of Happiness, put to him the question that interested them.

"Riches, and Honour," he said, "do not interest me, and even the most legitimate and natural affections, family ties, and the pleasures of friendship cannot fill my heart. I care for nothing but the public good; it is the unhappiest of passions, and the most cruelly thwarted of affections.

"I have enjoyed power; I have refused to support, with the funds of the Treasury and the blood of our soldiers, the expeditions organized by filibusters and merchants for their own enrichment, and the public ruin; I did not surrender the army and the fleet as a prey to contractors, and I was subjected to the calumnies of all the rogues who reproached me, amid the plaudits of the imbecile mob, with betraying the sacred interests and the glory of my mother country. No one has supported me against these high-class thieves. Seeing of what folly and cowardice popular opinion is compounded, I regret absolute power. The King's weakness drives me desperate; the littleness of the great is to me a disgusting spectacle; the incapacity and dishonesty of the ministers, and the ignorance, baseness, and venality of the people's representatives throw me alternately into fits of rage and stupor. To console myself for the ills which I endure by day I record them at night, and thus I disgorge the gall upon which I feed."

Quatrefeuilles and Saint-Sylvain raised their hats to the noble peer, and, walking a few steps down the gallery, they found themselves confronted by a very small man, apparently hump-backed, for his back was visible over his head. He was mincing along in a waddling conspicuous manner.

"It is useless to ask him," said Quatrefeuilles.

"Who knows?" said Saint-Sylvain.

"Believe me; I know him," replied the Equerry. "I am in his confidence. He is quite pleased with himself, and perfectly satisfied with his appearance; and he has reason to be so. That little hump-back is a favourite with the women. Ladies of the

Court and the city, actresses, merchants' wives, female rakes, cocottes, prudes, religious women—the proudest, the most beautiful are at his feet. In satisfying them, he is losing his health and even his life, and now, having fallen into a melancholy, he is enduring the burden of being a mascot."

The sun was setting, and learning that the King would not appear that day the last courtiers were quitting the apartments.

"I would gladly give my shirt," said Quatrefeuilles. "I may say that I have a happy temperament. Always contented, I drink, eat, and sleep well. I am complimented on my cheerful expression, and I am reckoned good looking; I have no complaint to make about my face. But I feel a weight and heat in the bladder, which take all the joy out of life. This morning I got rid of a stone as big as a pigeon's egg. I fear that my shirt would be of no value to the King."

"I would gladly give mine," said Saint-Sylvain, "but I also have a stone. It is my wife. I married the ugliest and most malicious creature that ever existed, and although we know that future is in God's hands, I make bold to assert that she is the ugliest and most malicious person that ever will exist, for the repetition of such an original is so highly improbable that one may regard it as impossible. There are some tricks which Nature never plays twice." Then leaving this painful subject, he said: "Quatrefeuilles, my friend, we have been lacking in judgment. It is not at Court, or among the mighty of this world, that we must search for a happy man."

"You speak like a philosopher," replied Quatrefeuilles. "You express yourself like that beggarly Jean-Jacques. You do yourself an injustice. There are just as many men who are happy, and worthy of being so, in the palaces of kings, and in the houses of the aristocracy, as in the cafés frequented by men of letters, or the cabarets to which the artisans resort. If we have not found a happy man to-day beneath this roof it is only because it is getting late, and we have not had a suitable chance. Let us visit the Queen's card-table to-night and we shall have better luck."

"Look for a happy man at a gaming table!" exclaimed Saint-Sylvain. "One might as well look for a pearl necklace in a turnip-field, or for truth in the mouth of a statesman! The Spanish Ambassador is giving a party to-night; the whole city will be there. Let us go thither, and we shall easily lay our hands on a good and suitable shirt."

"It has happened to me sometimes," said Quatrefeuilles, "to place my hand on the chemise of a happy woman. It was a real pleasure. But our happiness was but momentary. If I tell you this, it is not to boast (there is really no reason why I should), nor to recall past joys, which may return, for, contrary to the proverb, every age has the same pleasures. My intention is far different; it is more serious, and more virtuous, and refers directly to the august mission with which we are both entrusted: it is to submit to you an idea which has just come into my mind. Don't you think, Saint-Sylvain, that in prescribing the shirt of a happy man, Dr. Rodrigue was using the term 'man' in the generic sense, regarding the whole human species, without reference to sex, and meaning a woman's chemise as much as a man's shirt? For my part, I am inclined to believe it, and if you were of the same opinion we could extend the field of our researches and more than double our chances of success, for in a polished and elegant society such as our own, the women are happier than the men; we do more for them than they for us. Saint-Sylvain, our task being thus enlarged, we could divide it. Thus, for example, from to-night until to-morrow morning I could look for a happy woman while you were searching for a happy man. Admit, my friend, that a lady's chemise is a delicate article. I have already handled one that would pass through a ring; the batiste was finer than a cobweb. And what do you say, my friend, to that chemise which a lady at the Court of France, in the time of Marie-Antoinette, wore at a ball worked into her head-dress? We should deserve the King's gratitude, it seems to me, were we to present to the King our master a beautiful linen chemise, with insertions, Valenciennes trimmings, and magnificent rose ribbon shoulder-straps, lighter than a breath, and scented with fragrance of iris and of love."

But Saint-Sylvain protested vigorously against this interpretation of Dr. Rodrigue's prescription.

"What are you thinking of, Quatrefeuilles?" he cried. "A woman's chemise would only provide the King with a woman's happiness, which would be a source of shame and misery. I shall not at present consider the question, Quatrefeuilles, as to whether woman is more capable of happiness than man. This is neither the time nor the place; it is time to go to dinner. The physiologists attribute to women a more delicate sensibility than our own: but these are only transcendental generalities, which pass over people's heads, and do not take in anybody. I do not know whether, as you appear to believe, our polished society is better adapted for the happiness of women than for that of men. I notice that, in our world, they neither rear their children nor look after their homes; they know nothing, do nothing, and kill themselves with fatigue. They are consumed by shining; it is the fate of a candle. I do not know that it is an enviable condition. But that is not the question. Some day, perhaps, there will be only one sex; perhaps there may be three, or even more. In that case, sexual morality will be richer, fuller, and more varied. Meanwhile, we have two sexes; there is a good deal of each in the other, a good deal of man in the woman, and of woman in man. Still, they are distinct; they have each their nature, their habits, and their laws, their pleasures and their pains. If you were to emasculate his idea of happiness, with what a frozen gaze our King would thenceforward regard Madame de la Poule! Perhaps, indeed, owing to hypochondria and weakness, he might go so far as to compromise the honour of our glorious country. Is that what you wish, Quatrefeuilles?

"Cast your eyes, in the gallery of the Royal Palace, upon the history of Hercules, worked in Gobelin tapestry, and see what happened to that hero, who was particularly unfortunate in connection with chemises. For a jest he put on that of Omphale, and afterwards could only spin wool. That is the destiny which your imprudence is preparing for our illustrious monarch."

"Oh! oh!" said the First Equerry. "We will take it that I never mentioned it, and let us say no more about it."

CHAPTER IV

JERONIMO

THE Spanish Embassy blazed and twinkled in the night. The clouds were gilded by the reflection of its lights. Garlands of fire, edging the alleys of the park, gave the adjacent foliage the transparency and brilliancy of emeralds. Bengal fire reddened the sky above the lofty black trees. An invisible orchestra cast its voluptuous airs to the light breeze. The elegant crowd of guests covered the lawn ; dresses moved restlessly in the shadows ; military uniforms shone with crosses and orders ; bright figures glided gracefully over the grass, leaving a trail of perfume behind them.

Quatrefeuilles, seeing two illustrious statesmen, the President of the Council and his predecessor, talking together under the statue of Fortune, thought of accosting them. But Saint-Sylvain dissuaded him from his purpose.

"They are both unfortunate," he told him. "The one cannot console himself for having lost his power, and the other trembles lest he may lose it. And their ambition is yet the more pitiful in that they are both freer and more powerful in a private condition than while in the exercise of power, where they can only maintain themselves by a humble and dishonourable submission to the caprices of the Chambers, the blind passions of the people, and the interests of the financiers. What they are pursuing with such eagerness is nothing but their own pompous abasement. Ah! Quatrefeuilles, rest content with your prickers, your horses and your dogs, but do not aspire to govern men."

They passed on. Scarcely had they proceeded a few steps when, attracted by bursts of laughter issuing from a clump of trees, they entered the latter, and found, sitting on four chairs in an arbour, a fat man in disordered dress, who, in a mellow, emotional voice, was telling stories to a numerous company, which was hanging on his lips, that were like those of an ancient Satyr, and bending over his more or less than human face, which looked as if it had been smeared with Dionysiac lees. He was the most celebrated and only popular man in the kingdom, Jeronimo. He was speaking profusely, joyously, and richly; throwing off random remarks, and telling stories, some excellent, and others not so good, but all raising a laugh. He told a story of how one day at Athens, the social revolution took place, when all property was shared, and the women made in common. But the old and ugly ones very soon complained of being neglected, and a law was then passed in their favour, compelling the men to take their turn with them before passing on to the young and pretty ones. He described, with robust gaiety, comic espousals, grotesque embraces, and the failing courage of the young men at the appearance of their blear-eyed, snuffling mistresses, who looked capable of cracking nuts between their chins and noses. Then he told lewd tales of German Jews, priests, and peasants, a whole string of diverting stories and merry observations.

Jeronimo was an amazing oratorical instrument. When he spoke his whole person spoke, from his head to his feet: and never in any orator had the play of speech been so absolute. Grave and gay, sublime and ridiculous by turns, he was master of every form of eloquence, and the same man who, under the arbour, was relating, like the consummate comedian that he was, for the diversion of idlers, and his own, every kind of facetious anecdote, had, on the previous day, in the Chamber, raised an outcry and earned applause with his mighty voice, making the ministers tremble and the tribunes quake and stirring the whole country with the echoes of his speech. Dexterous in his violence, calculating in his outbursts of wrath, he had become leader of the Opposition, without falling out with those in power, and, working among the people, he associated with the aristocracy. He was referred to as the man of the period. He was the man of the hour; always his mind accommodated itself to the time and the place. His thoughts were always opportune; his gigantic and commonplace genius was in tune with that of the community; his prodigious mediocrity effaced all the greatness and the pettiness that surrounded him; he alone was to be seen. His health would of itself have assured him of happiness: it was as massive and robust as his soul. A great drinker, a great lover of flesh, whether roasted or alive, he took life joyously, and appropriated a lion's share of the pleasures of this world. Listening to him as he told his wonderful stories, Quatrefeuilles and Saint-Sylvain laughed like the rest, and, nudging the other's elbow, each gazed out the corner of his eye at the shirt over which Jeronimo had liberally scattered the sauces and wines of a mirthful feast.

The ambassador of a proud people, which was offering King Christophe, for a price, its interested friendship, was passing at this moment, magnificent and solitary, across the lawn. He went up to the great man, bowing to him slightly.

Immediately Jeronimo was transformed. A serene and gentle gravity, a sovereign calm spread over his countenance, and the restrained sonority of his voice flattered the ear of the ambassador, with the noblest and most caressing phrases of the language. His whole attitude expressed an understanding of foreign affairs, an atmosphere of congresses and conferences: his very lace scarf, his bulging shirt, and his elephantine trousers appeared miraculously to partake of the dignity of the diplomat and the atmosphere of embassies.

The guests moved away, and the two illustrious personages chatted for a long time in a friendly tone, appearing to be on a footing of intimacy which was widely remarked and commented upon by the politicians and the ladies of "the Service."

"Jeronimo," said one, "will be Minister of Foreign Affairs when he wishes."

"When he is," said another, "he will keep the King in his pocket."

The Austrian ambassador, examining him through his eyeglasses, said:

"That is an intelligent fellow; he will go far."

The conversation ended, Jeronimo took a turn round the garden with his faithful Jobelin, a sort of long-legged heron with the head of an owl, who never left him.

The private secretary and the First Equerry followed them.

"His is the shirt we want," said Quatrefeuilles in a low voice. "But will he give it to us? He is a Socialist, and against the King's Government."

"Bah!" said Saint-Sylvain. "He is not an ill-natured man, and he is witty. He cannot wish for any change, seeing that he is in opposition. He has no responsibility; his position is excellent; he must wish to retain it. A good member of the Opposition is always a Conservative. Unless I am very much mistaken, this demagogue would be very sorry to harm his King. If we negotiate skilfully we shall get his shirt. Like Mirabeau, he will treat with the Court. But he will have to be assured of secrecy."

As they were thus talking, Jeronimo was walking to and fro, with his hat over his ear, twirling his cane, diffusing his hilarious humour, jesting, bantering, laughing, exclaiming, playing on words, making obscene and filthy puns, and humming airs. Meanwhile, some fifteen paces ahead of him, the Duc des Aulnes, the arbiter of fashion and the prince of youth, meeting a lady of his acquaintance, saluted her very simply with a brief, slight, but not ungraceful gesture. The tribune observed him with an attentive gaze, and then becoming gloomy and thoughtful, he laid his heavy hand upon the shoulder of his water-fowl.

"Jobelin," he said, "I would give all my popularity and ten years of my life to wear a coat and speak to women as that young puppy does."

All his gaiety was gone. He now moved sadly

with lowered head, regarding without pleasure the shadow which the ironic moon cast between his legs like a grotesque bluish figure.

"What did he say? Is he joking?" asked Quatrefeuilles uneasily.

"Never in his life was he more serious, more sincere," replied Saint-Sylvain. "He has shown us the secret sore which devours him. Jeronimo cannot console himself for his lack of birth and elegance. He is not happy, and I would not give twopence for his shirt."

Time was slipping by, and the search was becoming burdensome. The private secretary and the First Equerry agreed to pursue their quest independently, and arranged to meet at supper in the small yellow salon in order to compare notes as to the result of their search. Quatrefeuilles, for choice, interrogated army officers, the great nobles, and the great landowners, but he did not forget to make inquiry among the women. Saint-Sylvain, of a more penetrating mind, read the eyes of financiers, and patted the backs of diplomatists.

They met at the hour agreed, both weary and with long faces.

"I saw nothing but happy people," said Quatrefeuilles, "but in every case their happiness was spoilt. The soldiers were consumed with a longing for a decoration, a step in rank or a gratuity. The benefits and honours gained by their rivals were like to give them jaundice. At the news that General de Tintille had been created Duc des Comores they were all as yellow as liquorice-water and as green as lizards. One became positively purple; it was a case of apoplexy. The nobility are dying of boredom and disturbances on their estates: always in litigation with their neighbours, eaten up by the lawyers, and their life of burdensome idleness is full of cares."

"I have found things no better than you have," said Saint-Sylvain. "And what strikes me is to find that people suffer from contrary causes, and for opposite reasons. I found the Prince des Estelles wretched because his wife is deceiving him; not that he loves her, but he has some self-respect; the Duc de Mauvert is miserable because his wife is not deceiving him, and is therefore depriving him of the means of restoring his ruined house. One man is worn out by his children, another is in despair because he has none. I met townsfolk who dream of nothing but living in the country, and country-folk who think of nothing but setting up in town. I received the confidences of two men of honour; one was inconsolable because he had killed in a duel the man who had stolen his mistress, and the other was in despair because he had missed his rival."

"I would never have believed," sighed Quatrefeuilles, "that it was so difficult to find a happy man."

"Perhaps we set about it the wrong way," objected Saint-Sylvain. "We are searching at random, without method; we do not precisely know what we are looking for. We have not defined Happiness. It must be defined."

"It would be waste of time," replied Quatrefeuilles.

"I beg your pardon," answered Saint-Sylvain. "When we shall have defined it, that is to say, limited, determined, and fixed it in its time and place, we shall have better means of finding it."

"I don't believe it," said Quatrefeuilles.

Still, they agreed to consult the wisest man in the kingdom on the subject. This was Monsieur Chaudesaigues, the Keeper of the King's Library.

When they re-entered the Palace the sun had already risen. Christophe V had passed a bad night, and was impatiently demanding the medicinal shirt. They apologized for the delay, and climbed to the third story, where Monsieur Chaudesaigues received them in a vast hall which contained eight hundred thousand printed volumes and manuscripts.

CHAPTER V

THE ROYAL LIBRARY

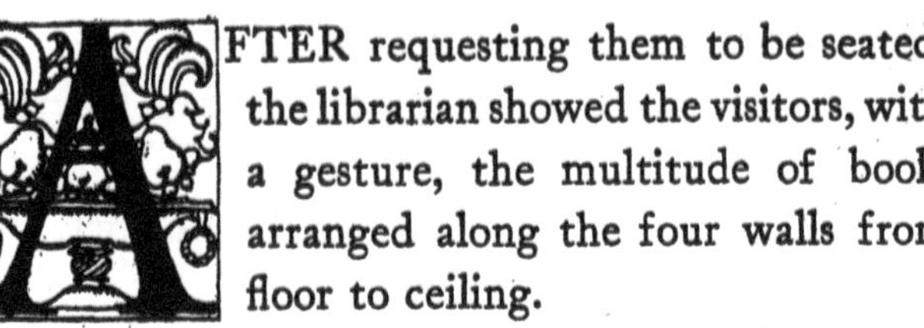

AFTER requesting them to be seated, the librarian showed the visitors, with a gesture, the multitude of books arranged along the four walls from floor to ceiling.

"Can't you hear? Can't you hear the uproar they make? My ears are bursting from it. They all talk at the same time, and in every language. They argue about everything: God, Nature, Man, Time, Space and Numbers, the Knowable and the Unknowable, Good and Evil; they examine and object to everything, affirm and deny everything. They reason; they contradict. There are light books and heavy books; cheerful books and melancholy books; diffuse books and concise books; many speak for the pleasure of saying nothing, counting syllables, arranging sounds in accordance with laws, whose meaning and origin they themselves ignore; they are the most self-satisfied. There are books of another kind, dismal and austere, which speculate only upon subjects which are devoid of any tangible quality, and are carefully divorced from natural contingencies; they argue in the void, restlessly moving through the invisible categories of space: there are rabid disputants, who maintain their entities and their symbols with a sanguinary fury. I will not linger over those that tell the history of their own times, or of former times, for no one believes them. In all, there are eight hundred thousand in this room, and there are not two that think precisely the same on any subject, and those that repeat each other do not agree among themselves. As a rule, they neither know what they themselves are saying nor what others have said.

"Gentlemen, as a result of listening to this universal clatter I shall go mad, as all those have done who dwelt before me in this hall of innumerable voices, unless they were naturally idiots when they came, like my venerable colleague, Monsieur Froidefond, whom you see sitting opposite me, cataloguing with peaceful ardour. Simple he was born, and simple he remains. He was a complete unity, and has not become various. For unity cannot produce diversity, and it is there, I would remind you in passing, gentlemen, that the first difficulty is encountered, when we seek for the origin of things: it being impossible that the cause should be unique, it must be double, triple, or multiple, which is difficult to admit. Monsieur Froidefond has a simple mind, and a pure soul. He lives catalogically. He knows the title and the *format* of every book which adorns these walls, and thus possesses the only exact knowledge which it is possible to acquire in a library. Having never investigated the contents of a single book, he has been saved from the nerveless uncertainty, hydra-headed error, hideous doubt, and horrible uneasiness, monsters which reading engenders in a fertile brain. He is calm, peaceful, and happy."

"Happy!" simultaneously exclaimed the two seekers after the shirt.

"He is happy," replied Monsieur Chaudesaigues, "but he does not know it. And it may be that one can be happy only on that condition."

"Alas," said Saint-Sylvain, "it is not life to be unaware that one lives; one is not happy if one does not know it."

But Quatrefeuilles, who mistrusted argument, and believed only in experience in all things, went up to the table where Froidefond was busy cataloguing. He was surrounded by a heap of volumes, bound in calf, sheepskin, morocco, vellum, parchment, pigskin and boards; they smelt of dust and mildew, rats and mice.

"Worthy librarian," he said, "kindly answer me this question. Are you happy?"

"I know of no book under that title," replied the old cataloguer.

Quatrefeuilles raised his hands as a token of discouragement, and resumed his place.

"Reflect, gentlemen," said Chaudesaigues, "that the antique Cybele, bearing Monsieur Froidefond upon her blooming bosom, is causing him to describe an immense curve round the sun, and that the sun is drawing Monsieur Froidefond with the earth, and all its retinue of planets, across the voids of space, toward the constellation of Hercules. Why? Of the eight hundred thousand volumes assembled around us not one can tell us why. We are ignorant of that, and of everything else. Gentlemen, we know nothing. The causes of our ignorance are many, but I am convinced that the most important is the imperfection of language. The torrent of words produces confusion among our ideas. If we took more care to define the terms by means of which we reason our ideas would be clearer and more certain."

"What did I tell you, Quatrefeuilles?" cried the triumphant Saint-Sylvain. And, turning to the librarian, he said: "Monsieur Chaudesaigues, what you have just said fills me with joy. And I see that in coming to you we have been well advised. We have come to ask you for a definition of Happiness. It is on His Majesty's service——"

"I will do the best I can. The definition of a word should be radical and etymological. You ask me what is understood by 'bonheur'? 'Bonheur' or heur bon, is good augury, the favourable omen derived from the flight and the song of birds, in opposition to 'malheur,' or 'mauvais heur,' which signifies an unfavourable consultation; the word indicates as much."

"But how," asked Quatrefeuilles, "can one find out if a man is happy?"

"By the examination of chickens!" answered the librarian. "The word implies it. 'Heur' is derived from *augurium*, which is a corruption of *avigurium*."

"The examination of sacred chickens has ceased since the time of the Romans," objected the First Equerry.

"But," asked Saint-Sylvain, "is not a happy man one to whom fortune is favourable, and do not certain outward and visible signs of good fortune exist?"

"Fortune," answered Chaudesaigues, "is that which befalls of good or ill; it is a throw of the dice. If I understand you rightly, gentlemen, you are looking for a happy man, a lucky man, that is to say a man for whom the birds have none but favourable auguries, and whom the dice always befriend. You must search for this rare mortal among men whose life is drawing to a close, and for preference among those already stretched upon their death-bed, who will have no further need to consult the sacred chickens, nor to throw dice. For they alone are in a position to congratulate themselves upon a constant good fortune, and unvarying happiness.

"Did not Sophocles say in his *Œdipus Rex*, 'Call no man happy till his hour of death?'"

This advice ill-suited Quatrefeuilles, to whom the idea did not appeal of pursuing happiness in the train of the Holy Sacrament. Neither did the plan of dragging a shirt off a dying man commend itself to Saint-Sylvain; but as he was possessed of some philosophy and curiosity he asked the librarian if he knew of one of these grand old men who have for the last time cast their splendidly cogged dice.

Chaudesaigues nodded his head and rose, went to the window, and drummed on the panes. It was raining; the parade-ground was deserted. At the far end there rose a magnificent palace, whose attics were surmounted by a trophy of arms, and which bore upon its pediment a Bellona, a hydra upon her helmet, clad in a cuirass of scales, and brandishing a Roman sword.

"Go into that palace," he said at length.

"What?" said Saint-Sylvain, surprised, "to the Marshal de Volmar's?"

"To be sure. What mortal under the sky is more fortunate than the conqueror of Elbrüz and Baskir? Volmar is one of the greatest fighting men that ever lived, and, of all, the most uniformly lucky."

"The whole world knows that," said Quatrefeuilles.

"And will never forget it," resumed the librarian.

Marshal Pilon, Duc de Volmar, coming into the world at a period when popular conflagrations were no longer consuming the whole face of the world simultaneously, was able to correct this ingratitude of fortune by throwing himself with all his energy and genius into any point of the globe where a war was on the point of blazing forth. At the age of twelve he served in Turkey, and went through the Kurdistan campaign. From that time forth he had borne his victorious arms into every portion of the known world; four times he had crossed the Rhine, with such insolent ease that the old reed-crowned river, the divider of peoples, seemed flouted and abashed: he had defended the line of the Lys even more skilfully than Marshal Saxe; he had crossed the Pyrenees, forced the entrance of the Tagus, opened the gates of the Caucasus, and ascended the Dnieper. He had, in turn, faced and fought every nation of Europe, and had three times saved his country.

CHAPTER VI

MARSHAL THE DUC DE VOLMAR

CHAUDESAIGUES sent for the campaigns of the Duc de Volmar. Three library attendants bowed beneath the burden. The tables were lost to sight under the opened atlases.

"Here, gentlemen, are the campaigns of Styria, the Palatinate, Karamania, the Caucasus, and the Vistula. The marches and positions of the armies are exactly indicated on the maps by lozenges and pretty little flags; the order of battle is perfectly shown. This order is generally determined after a battle, and it is the genius of great captains to erect into a system, to their own glory, the whims of hazard. But the Duc de Volmar has always foreseen everything.

"Cast your eyes on this plan, on a scale of one ten-thousandth, of the famous battle of Baskir, won by Volmar against the Turks. He there displayed the most amazing tactical genius. The action commenced at 5 a.m.; at 4 p.m. Volmar's troops, overwhelmed by fatigue, their ammunition exhausted, were falling back in disorder. The intrepid

Marshal, alone at the bridgehead of the Aluta, with a pistol in either hand, was blowing out the brains of the runaways. He was planning his retreat when he learned that the enemy, in full flight, was throwing itself desperately into the Danube. Immediately he faced about, flung himself in pursuit of them, and achieved their destruction. That victory earned him a pension of five hundred thousand francs, and opened for him the doors of the Institute.

"Gentlemen, do you think you can find a man happier than the victor of Elbrüz and Baskir? With unvarying good fortune he has fought fourteen campaigns, won sixty pitched battles, and three times saved his grateful country from total ruin. Loaded with glory and honours, he is prolonging beyond the ordinary term of life, in wealth and peace, an august old age."

"It is true; he is fortunate," said Quatrefeuilles. "What do you think about it, Saint-Sylvain?"

"Let us ask for an interview," said the private secretary.

Admitted to the Palace, they crossed the hall where stood the Marshal's equestrian statue.

On the pedestal were inscribed these proud words: "I bequeath my two daughters, Elbrüz and Baskir, to the gratitude of my country, and the admiration of the world."

The state staircase raised its double curve of marble steps between walls decorated with trophies and flags. Its wide landing led to a door whose two leaves were adorned with trophies of arms and smoking grenades, surmounted by the three golden crowns bestowed by King, Parliament, and Nation on the Duc de Volmar, saviour of his country.

Saint-Sylvain and Quatrefeuilles halted, frozen by a sense of awe, before the closed door; at the thought of the hero from whom it divided them emotion nailed them to the threshold, and they dared not venture to face so much glory.

Saint-Sylvain recalled the medal struck in commemoration of the battle of Elbrüz, which showed on the obverse the Marshal placing a crown on the brows of a winged victory, with the following magnificent inscription: "*Victoria Cæsarem et Napoleonem coronavit; major autem Volmarus coronat Victoriam.*"

And he murmured:

"This man is a hundred cubits high."

Quatrefeuilles pressed both hands to his heart, which was beating as though it would burst.

Hardly had they collected their thoughts when they heard sharp cries, which seemed to issue from the far end of the apartments, and to be gradually approaching. They were the screams of a woman, mingled with the sound of blows, and followed by feeble moans. The doors suddenly flew open, and a very little old man, kicked forward by a powerful serving wench, collapsed on the stairs like a marionette, rolled down the staircase head first, and fell, bruised, broken, and dislocated into the hall, before the solemn footmen. It was the Duc de Volmar. They picked him up. The maid-servant with dishevelled hair and uncovered bosom, shouted from above:

"Leave him alone! He's only fit to be touched with a broom." Brandishing a bottle, she continued: "He wanted to take away my brandy! By what right? Get out, you old ruin! It wasn't me that was wanting you, that's very certain, you old carrion!"

Quatrefeuilles and Saint-Sylvain fled hastily from the Palace. When they reached the parade-ground Saint-Sylvain made the remark that the hero's latest throw of the dice had not been a lucky one.

"Quatrefeuilles," he added, "I see that I have been mistaken. I wished to proceed by an exact and rigorous method—I was wrong. Science leads us astray. Let us return to common sense. For satisfactory guidance one must rely on the crudest empiricism. Let us search for happiness without trying to define it."

Quatrefeuilles launched into lengthy recriminations and abuse of the librarian, whom he regarded as a malicious jester. What annoyed him most was to feel that his faith was destroyed, that the worship which he had paid in his heart to the national hero was debased and soiled. This pained him. His was a generous grief, and doubtless generous griefs contain their own consolation, and, so to speak, their recompense: they are better and more easily endured and with a readier courage than egotistical and selfish sorrows. It would be unjust to wish that it should be otherwise. So that Quatrefeuilles' heart was very soon sufficiently at leisure, and his mind sufficiently clear, to perceive that the rain was falling on his silk hat, and damaging its lustre, and he sighed:

"Another hat ruined."

He had been a soldier, and had formerly served his King as a lieutenant of dragoons. Thus it was that an idea occurred to him. He proceeded to buy, at the library of the General Staff, on the parade-ground, at the corner road leading to the great stables, a map of the kingdom and a plan of the capital.

"One should never start on a campaign without maps," he said. "But the devil of it is to read them. Here is the city with its suburbs. Where shall we begin? In the north, south, east, or west? It has been remarked that all cities spread westwards. Perhaps this affords us a hint which we should not neglect. It is possible that the dwellers in the western area, sheltered from the keen east wind, enjoy better health, have a more even temper, and are happier. Or rather, let us begin with the charming slopes rising from the bank of the river some thirty miles south of the city. The wealthiest families in the country live there at this time of the year. And whatever anyone may say, it is among the fortunate that we must look for a happy man."

"Quatrefeuilles," answered the private secretary, "I am not an enemy of society, neither am I opposed to public happiness. I will speak of the rich as an honest man, and a good citizen. The rich are worthy of love and veneration. While making further additions to their wealth, they support the State, and are benefactors even without intending it, for they feed a multitude of people who are occupied in the preservation and increase of their property. Oh! what a beautiful, worthy, and excellent thing is private wealth! How it should be considered, disburdened, and privileged by the wise legislator, and what an iniquitous, perfidious, disloyal thing it is, how contrary to the most sacred rights and the worthiest of interests, and disastrous and fatal to public finance to injure opulence! It is a social duty to believe in the virtue of the wealthy: it is also pleasant to believe in their happiness. Quatrefeuilles, let us proceed!"

CHAPTER VII

THE CONNECTION BETWEEN WEALTH AND HAPPINESS

EING resolved to apply first of all to the best and richest, Jacques Felgine-Cobur, who owned mountains of gold, mines of diamonds, and seas of petroleum, they followed for a long time the walls of his park, which enclosed immense meadows, forests, farms, and villages; at every gate of the demesne at which they presented themselves they were sent on to another. Tired of continually going backwards and forwards, and incessantly winding about, they saw, in the road, a road-mender breaking stones in front of a grille with armorial bearings, and asked him if that was the gate through which they would reach the residence of Monsieur Jacques Felgine-Cobur, whom they wished to see.

The man painfully straightened out his bony back, and turned towards them his sunken face, protected by wire goggles.

"I am Monsieur Jacques Felgine-Cobur," he said.

Noticing their surprise, he continued :

" I break stones ; it is my only amusement."

Then bending down again he struck a pebble with his hammer. It broke with a sharp crack.

As they moved off Saint-Sylvain said :

" He is too rich. His fortune is crushing him ; he is unhappy."

Quatrefeuilles was of opinion they might next call upon Jacques Felgine-Cobur's rival, Joseph Machero, the iron king, whose brand-new château stood abhorrent upon a neighbouring hill, with its crenelated towers, and its walls pierced with machicolations bristling with watch-towers. Saint-Sylvain dissuaded him.

" You have seen his portrait ; he looks pitiable ; we know from the papers that he is full of piety, lives like a pauper, preaches to little boys, and sings psalms in church. Rather let us go and see the Prince de Lusance. He is a true aristocrat, who knows how to enjoy his money. He shuns the turmoil of business, and does not go to Court. He is a lover of gardens, and has the finest picture-gallery in the kingdom."

They were announced. The Prince de Lusance received them in his cabinet of antiquities, where was to be seen the finest known Greek copy of the Cnidian Aphrodite, the work of a chisel worthy of Praxiteles, and full of beauty. The goddess appeared still wet from the waves of the sea. A rosewood cabinet, which had belonged to Madame de Pompadour, contained the finest gold and silver coins of Greece and Sicily. The Prince, a fine judge, was himself drawing up a catalogue of his medals. His magnifying glass was still lingering over the glass case containing the engraved stones, jasper, onyx, sardonyx, and chalcedony, containing within the area of a finger-nail figures modelled in a large style, and groups composed with a magnificent breadth of feeling. With a loving hand, he took from his table a little bronze faun that his visitors might admire its contours and its patina. His language was worthy of the masterpiece which he was describing.

"I am awaiting," he said, "a consignment of antique silver, of cups and bowls, which are said to be more beautiful than those of Hildesheim and Bosco-reale! I am impatient to see them. Monsieur de Caylus knew no greater pleasure than that of opening cases. I am of his opinion."

Saint-Sylvain smiled.

"Nevertheless, my dear Prince, you are said to be an expert in all the pleasures."

"You flatter me, Monsieur de Saint-Sylvain. But I believe that the art of pleasure is the first of all arts, and that the rest are valueless except in so far as they minister to it."

He conducted his guests to the picture gallery, where were mingled the silvery tones of Veronese, the ambers of Titian, the reds of Rubens and Rembrandt, and the greys and roses of Velasquez; where the chorus of palettes formed a glorious harmony. A violin, lay forgotten on a chair before the portrait of a dark lady, with smooth-tressed hair and an olive complexion; her great chestnut eyes were the notable feature of her face. It was some unknown woman whose lines Ingres had caressed with a sure and loving hand.

"I will confess my ruling folly," said the Prince de Lusance. "Sometimes, when alone, I play before these pictures, and enjoy the illusion of translating into sound the harmony of line and colour. Before this portrait I try to convey the firm caress of the drawing, and, full of discouragement, I abandon my violin."

A window opened on to the park. The Prince and his guests leant upon the balcony.

"What a beautiful view!" said Quatrefeuilles and Saint-Sylvain.

Terraces, covered with statues, orange trees and flowers, led down by easy, gradual steps to the lawn edged with yoke-elms, and the fountains whence the water leaped up in white spouts from the conch-shells of Tritons and the urns of nymphs. Right and left spread a sea of verdure stretched in peaceful undulations to the distant river, whose silver thread could be followed among the poplars, under hills enveloped in rosy mists.

But lately smiling, the Prince directed a worried look toward a point in the vast and beautiful landscape.

"That chimney!" he murmured in a pained voice, pointing with his finger to a smoking factory chimney, more than half a league from the park.

"That chimney? One can hardly see it," said Quatrefeuilles.

"I see nothing else," replied the Prince. "For me, it spoils the whole view, the whole of nature, the whole of my life. The evil is beyond remedy. It belongs to a company which will not abandon its factory at any price. I have tried every means of hiding it, and have failed. It is making me ill."

And, leaving the window, he threw himself into an arm-chair.

"We should have foreseen it," said Quatrefeuilles, as they got in their carriage. "He is fastidious and unhappy."

Before resuming their search they sat for a moment in the little garden of an inn which stood on the summit of the hill, whence they could see the beautiful valley and the clear winding river, with its oval islets. In spite of two desperate failures they still hoped to find a happy millionaire.

There yet remained a dozen in the country; amongst others, Monsieur Bloch, Monsieur Potiquet, Baron Nichol, the greatest manufacturer in the kingdom, and the Marquis de Granthosme, perhaps the richest of all, a member of an illustrious family, and as heavily loaded with honours as with wealth.

Near them a tall, thin man, bent double, and as limp as a bolster, was drinking a cup of milk; his great pale eyes were sunk deep in his cheeks; and his nose hung over his mouth. He appeared to be in the very depths of woe, and stared with distress at Quatrefeuilles' boots.

After gazing at them for twenty minutes he rose, dismal and resolute, approached the First Equerry, and, apologizing for his importunity, said:

"Sir, allow me to ask a question which to me is of the greatest importance. How much do you pay for your boots?"

"Despite the peculiarity of your request," answered Quatrefeuilles, "I see no objection to answering it. I paid sixty-five francs for this pair."

For a long time the stranger alternately examined his own foot and that of his interlocutor, comparing the two boots with minute attention.

Then, pale, and with a voice full of emotion, he said:

"You say you paid sixty-five francs for those boots. Are you perfectly sure?"

"Why, certainly."

"Sir, I beg you to be careful what you say."

"Come, come," muttered Quatrefeuilles, who was beginning to get annoyed, "you are a curious sort of bootmaker, sir!"

"I am not a bootmaker," replied the stranger, with gentle humility. "I am the Marquis de Granthosme."

Quatrefeuilles saluted him.

"Sir," continued the Marquis, "I felt it: alas, I am still being robbed! You pay for your boots sixty-five francs; I pay for mine, precisely like yours, eighty-five francs. It is not the money that I consider; the price is no object to me, but I cannot endure being robbed. I see and breathe nothing around me but fraud, dishonesty, theft, and falsehood. I have a horror of my wealth, which corrupts all who comes near me—servants, stewards, contractors, neighbours, friends, wife and children. It makes me odious and contemptible to them. Mine is a cruel situation. I am never certain that the man before me is not dishonest. I feel ready to die of disgust and shame at being a member of the human species."

And the Marquis seized his glass of milk, gasping:

"Sixty-five francs! Sixty-five francs!"

At this moment groans and lamentations burst forth on the road, and the King's two emissaries saw an old man, who was whining, followed by two gold-laced lackeys.

They were perturbed by the sight; but the innkeeper was quite indifferent.

"It is nothing," he told them. "It's only the rich Baron Nichol! He has gone mad, believes himself ruined, and goes lamenting day and night."

"Baron Nichol!" cried Saint-Sylvain. "Yet another of those whose shirt you wished to ask for, Quatrefeuilles."

After this last encounter, they abandoned any further quest of the health-giving shirt among the very rich of the kingdom.

As they were disappointed with their day's work, and feared to be ill received at the Palace, they laid the blame on each other for their mistakes.

"What was your idea, Quatrefeuilles, in going among those people with any other object than the observation of abnormalities? There is nothing sane, nothing normal about them, whether their morals, ideas or sensations. They are all monsters."

"What! Did you not say, Saint-Sylvain, that wealth was a virtue, that it was right to believe in the excellence of the wealthy, and delightful to believe in their happiness? But have a care: there is wealth and wealth. When the nobility is poor and the commonalty rich the State is overturned, and it is the end of everything."

"Quatrefeuilles, I am sorry to have to say it, but you have no notion of the constitution of modern states. You do not understand the period in which you live. However, that does not matter. Suppose we were now to try gilded mediocrity? What do you think of that? I think we should be wise in attending to-morrow the receptions of the ladies of the city, both middle-class and titled. We shall have an opportunity of observing people of every condition, and, if you agree with me, we will first of all visit middle-class folks in a modest position."

CHAPTER VIII

THE SALONS OF THE CAPITAL

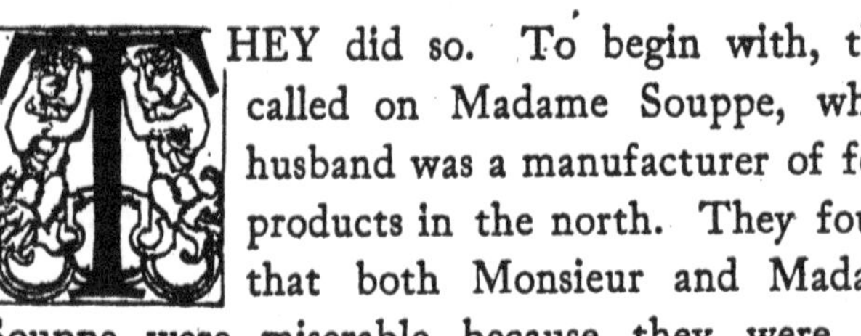

THEY did so. To begin with, they called on Madame Souppe, whose husband was a manufacturer of food products in the north. They found that both Monsieur and Madame Souppe were miserable because they were not received by Madame Esterlin, whose husband was an ironmaster, and a Member of Parliament.

They went to Madame Esterlin's, and found her in great distress, and Monsieur Esterlin as well, because they were not received by Madame du Colombier, whose husband was a peer of the realm, and late Minister of Justice. When they came to Madame Colombier's house they found both the peer and his lady furious because they were not intimate with the Queen.

The visitors whom they met in these several houses were no less unhappy, disappointed or angry. Sickness, or wounded affection, or money troubles were consuming them. Those who possessed, and feared to lose, were even more unfortunate than those who had nothing. The obscure wished to shine, and the celebrities to shine yet more. The greater number were overwhelmed with work; and those who had nothing to do suffered a boredom more merciless than toil. Many of them pitied and felt the pains of others; they suffered with the sufferings of a wife or a beloved child. Many were declining under an illness from which they were not suffering, but which they believed they had contracted, or feared they might contract.

A cholera epidemic had just been raging in the capital, and a financier was mentioned who, fearing to be attacked by the contagion, and knowing of no sufficiently safe refuge, committed suicide.

"The worst of it is," said Quatrefeuilles, "that all these people, not content with the real evils which are pelting them like hailstones, plunge into a bog of imaginary misfortunes."

"There are no imaginary misfortunes," answered Saint-Sylvain. "All evils are real as soon as one feels them, and the dream of sorrow is a genuine sorrow."

"Well," replied Quatrefeuilles, "when I pass a stone as big as a duck's egg, I could wish it were only a dream."

Once more Saint-Sylvain observed that men

often plague themselves for opposite and contrary reasons.

In Madame du Colombier's drawing-room he conversed in succession with two men of great intelligence, enlightened and cultivated, who by the twists and turns which they unconsciously gave to their thoughts, revealed to him the moral evil by which they were deeply attacked. It was from the state of public affairs that both derived the cause of their anxiety, but they derived it in diametrically opposite ways. Monsieur Brome lived in perpetual fear of a change. In the present stability, and in the midst of the peace and prosperity which the country was now enjoying, he dreaded disorders and feared a complete upheaval. He opened the papers with trembling hands: every morning he expected to find in them the news of riots and disturbances. Suffering under this impression, he magnified the most ordinary and insignificant incidents into preludes of revolution and forerunners of cataclysms. Believing himself always on the eve of a universal catastrophe he lived in perpetual terror.

Monsieur Sandrique, on the other hand, was eaten up by a stranger and more uncommon malady. Tranquillity bored him, public order annoyed him; peace was odious to him, and the sublime monotony of human and divine laws overwhelmed him. He called secretly for change, and feigning to fear them, he sighed for catastrophes. This good, kindly, pleasant creature could conceive no other amusement than the violent subversion of his country, of the world, of the universe; watching even the stars for collisions and conflagrations. Disappointed, despondent, melancholy, morose, when the tone of the papers and the aspect of the streets showed him the unchanging peaceableness of the nation, he suffered all the more thereby, because, owing to his knowledge of men and his experience of public business, he knew how firmly entrenched in the peoples are the spirit of conservation and the tradition of imitation and obedience, and how slowly and with how equal a pace the social system progressed.

At Madame du Colombier's reception Saint-Sylvain noted another contradiction, even greater and more important.

In a corner of the little drawing-room, Monsieur de La Galissonière, President of the Civil Court, was conversing peacefully, and in a low voice, with Monsieur Larive-du-Mont, administrator of the Zoological Gardens.

"I will confess, my friend," said Monsieur de La Galissonière, "that the idea of death is simply killing me. I never stop thinking of it, and am dying of it. Death terrifies me not of itself, for it is nothing, but because of what follows after, the future life. I am a believer; I have faith in the certainty of my immortality. Reason, instinct, science, and revelation all demonstrate the existence of an imperishable soul; all prove to me that the nature, the origin and the ends of man are as they are taught by the Church. I am a Christian, and believe in eternal punishment; and the terrible idea of this punishment incessantly pursues me. I fear hell, and this fear, stronger than any other feeling, destroys my hope and all the virtues necessary to salvation, throws me into despair, and exposes me to the reprobation which I dread. I am damned by the fear of damnation, I am cast into hell by the dread of it, and, still living, I suffer eternal torments in advance. There is no punishment comparable to that which I am enduring, and which becomes acuter from year to year, from day to day, from hour to hour, since every day and every minute brings me nearer to that which I dread. My life is one agony full of fears and horrors."

As he spoke the magistrate beat the air with his hands, as if to ward off the undying flames by which he felt surrounded.

"My dear friend, I envy you," sighed Monsieur Larive-du-Mont. "Compared with me, you are a happy man. The idea of death rends me also; but how that idea differs from yours, and how far it surpasses it in horror! I am only too firmly persuaded by my studies and observations, by the continuous practice of comparative anatomy, and by deep research into the constitution of matter, that the words soul, spirit, immortality, spirituality, represent merely physical phenomena, or their negation, and that, for us, the limit of life is also that of consciousness, seeing that death consummates our complete destruction. There is no word to express what follows life, for the term nothingness which we employ is merely a sign of denial before the whole of nature. Nothingness is an infinite nothing, and by this we are enveloped. Thence we came, and thither we shall return; we are like a shell on the sea, between two voids.

"Nothingness is at once the impossible, and the certain: it cannot be conceived, yet it exists. The misery of man, and his crime, look you, lies in having discovered these things. The other animals do not know them: we should have ignored them for ever. To be, and cease to be! The horror of this idea makes my hair stand on end; it never leaves me. For me that which will not be spoils and corrupts that which is: the void swallows me by anticipation. Wicked absurdity! I feel myself, I see myself there."

"I am more to be pitied than you," said Monsieur de La Galissonière. "Every time you pronounce that false and delicious word, nothingness, its sweetness soothes my soul, and promises me, like a sick man's pillow, sleep and rest."

But Larive-du-Mont answered:

"My sufferings are more unbearable than yours, for the vulgar support the idea of eternal hell-fire, while an uncommon strength of mind is required to be an atheist. A religious training and a mystical bent of mind have given you the fear and hatred of human life. Not only are you a Christian and a Catholic; you are also a Jansenist, you carry at your side the abyss which Pascal skirted. For my part, I love life, this earthly life, life as it is, this dirty life. I love it, brutal, base, and coarse; I love it, sordid, filthy, and spoiled; I love it, stupid, imbecile, and cruel; I love it in its obscenity, in its ignominy, in its infamy, with all its stains, its stinks, its deformities, its corruptions and its infections. Feeling that it is escaping and eluding me, I tremble like a coward, and become mad with despair.

"On Sundays and holidays I wander through the populous parts of the town, mixing with the crowd in the streets, plunging into the groups of men, women, and children round the street singers, or before the showmen's booths. I rub up against dirty petticoats and greasy blouses; I inspire the heavy, warm odours of breath and sweat and hair. It seems to me that in this swarming life I feel further from death. I hear a voice saying:

"'I alone shall cure you of the fear which I inspire; I alone shall give you rest from the weariness with which my threats overwhelm you.'

"But I don't want it, I don't want it!"

"Alas!" said the magistrate. "If we do not cure in this world the evils by which our souls are ruined, death will bring us no peace."

"And what infuriates me," resumed the scientist, "is that when we are both dead, I shall not even have the satisfaction of saying: 'You see, La Galissonière, I was not mistaken; there is nothing.' I shall not enjoy the pleasure of having been right. And you will never be undeceived. At what a price is thought repaid! You are unhappy, my friend, because your mind is stronger and more capacious than that of the animals, and the majority of men. And I am unhappier than you because I have greater genius."

Quatrefeuilles, who had caught scraps of this conversation, was not greatly impressed.

"These are mental troubles," he said. "They may be acute, but they are uncommon. I am more alarmed by the more ordinary woes, sufferings, and deformities of the body, disappointments in love, and lack of money, which make our search so difficult."

"Besides," observed Saint-Sylvain, "those two gentlemen are too urgent in forcing their doctrine to make them miserable. If La Galissonière were to consult a good Jesuit father he would soon be reassured, and Larive-du-Mont ought to know that one can be an atheist with serenity like Lucretius, or with enjoyment, like André Chénier. He should repeat the verse of Homer: 'Patroclus is dead, who was worth more than you,' and consent with better grace some day to join his masters, the philosophers of antiquity, the humanists of the Renaissance, the modern scholars, and so many others of greater worth than himself. 'Paris and Helen are dead,' said François Villon. 'We are all mortal,' said Cicero. 'We all die,' said that woman whom wisdom the Holy Scripture praised in the Second Book of Kings."

CHAPTER IX

THE HAPPINESS OF BEING LOVED

THEY went to dine in the Royal Park, a fashionable promenade, which is in the capital of King Christophe what the Bois de Boulogne is in Paris, the Cambre in Brussels, Hyde Park in London, the Thiergarten in Berlin, the Prater in Vienna, the Prado in Madrid, the Cascine in Florence, and the Pincio in Rome. Seated in the open air, amidst the brilliant crowd of diners, their eyes wandered over the great hats covered with flowers and feathers, roving canopies of pleasure, moving screens of love, dovecotes to which desire winged its way.

"I believe," said Quatrefeuilles, "that what we are looking for is here. I have been loved, like every one else: that was Happiness, Saint-Sylvain: and once more I ask myself whether this is not man's only happiness; and although I carry the weight of a bladder more loaded with stones than a waggon coming out of a quarry, there are days when I feel as full of love as when I was twenty."

"I," answered Saint-Sylvain, "am a misogynist. I cannot forgive women for being of the same sex as Madame de Saint-Sylvain. They are all, I know, less foolish, less malignant, and less ugly, but it is too much that they should have something in common with her."

"Never mind that, Saint-Sylvain. I repeat that what we are looking for is here, and that we have only to stretch out our hands to grasp it."

Pointing to a handsome man sitting alone at a little table, he said:

"You know Jacques de Navicelle. He pleases women, all women. That is happiness, or I don't know what is."

Saint-Sylvain was of opinion that they had better make sure.

They invited Jacques de Navicelle to join their table, and as they dined they chatted with him in a familiar fashion. Twenty times, by circuitous approaches, or sharp turns, by frontal or flank attack, by insinuation, or perfectly frankly, they endeavoured to learn whether he was happy, without being able to learn anything about their companion, whose cultivated conversation and charming features expressed neither joy nor sorrow. Jacques de Navicelle talked freely, showing himself open and natural; he even indulged in confidences, but they concealed his secret, and left him all the more impenetrable. There was no doubt but that he was loved; was he happy or unhappy? By the time the fruit was brought the King's two inquisitors gave up hope of learning. Fatigued by their campaign, they talked idly, and about themselves; Saint-Sylvain about his wife, and Quatrefeuilles about his stone, in which he resembled Montaigne. They exchanged stories as they drank their liqueurs: the story of Madame Bérille, who slipped out of a private room, disguised as a pastry-cook's boy, with a basket on her head; the story of General Debonnaire, and the Baroness de Bildermann; the story of Monsieur Vizire and Madame Cérés, who, like Antony and Cleopatra, squandered an empire in kisses, and many others, old and new. Jacques de Navicelle told a story of the East.

"There was a young merchant of Bagdad, who lying one morning on his bed, felt full of love, and, with loud exclamations, prayed that he might be beloved of all women. A djinn who overheard him appeared to him and said:

"'Your desire is already accomplished. From this day forth you will be beloved by all women.'" Immediately the young merchant leapt joyfully from his bed, and, promising himself varied and inexhaustible pleasures, went down into the street. He had hardly gone a few steps when a horrible old woman, who was filtering wine in a cellar, blew him kisses through the grating. He averted his head in disgust, but the old woman caught him by the leg, dragged him into the cellar, and there kept him a prisoner for twenty years."

As Jacques de Navicelle was finishing the story, a waiter came up to tell him that some one was asking for him. He rose, and with dull eye and hanging head strolled off to the gate of the garden, where, sitting back in a coupé, a somewhat forbidding figure was awaiting him.

"He has just been telling us his own story," said Saint-Sylvain. "The young merchant of Bagdad is himself."

Quatrefeuilles struck his forehead.

"Some one told me that he was guarded by a dragon. I had forgotten it."

They returned late to the Palace with no other shirts but their own. They found King Christophe and Madame de la Poule weeping bitterly as they listened to a sonata by Mozart.

Owing to association with the King, Madame de la Poule suffered from melancholia, nursing gloomy ideas and foolish terrors. She believed herself to be persecuted, and the victim of abominable schemes. She lived in perpetual fear of being poisoned, and obliged her maids to taste all her food. She was terrified of death, and the attraction of suicide. The King's condition was aggravated by that of the lady, with whom he passed melancholy days.

"Painters," said Christophe V, "are sad artificers of imposture. They lend a touching beauty to weeping women, and show us an Andromache, an Artemis, a Magdalenes, and an Héloise adorned by their tears. I have a portrait of Adrienne Lecouvreur in the rôle of Cornelia, watering with her tears the ashes of Pompey; she is adorable. Directly Madame de la Poule begins to cry, her face screws up, her nose becomes red, and she is ugly enough to frighten you."

The unhappy Prince, who was living only in expectation of the health-giving shirt, abused Quatrefeuilles and Saint-Sylvain for their neglect, incapacity, and bad luck, reckoning that, of these three charges, one at least would be just.

"You will let me die, like my doctors, Saumon and Machellier. But that's their profession. From you I hoped better things; I relied on your devotion and intelligence. I see that I was mistaken. Are you not ashamed to return empty-handed? Was your mission so difficult to fulfil? Is it then so hard to find the shirt of a happy man? If you are not even capable of that, of what use are you? One is never well served unless by oneself. It is true of private individuals, and still truer of kings.

I shall go at once myself and look for this shirt which you cannot find."

Throwing off his night-cap and dressing-gown, he asked for his clothes.

Quatrefeuilles and Saint-Sylvain endeavoured to restrain him.

"Sire, how rash, in your condition."

"Sire, it has struck midnight."

"Do you then think that happy folk go to bed like hens?" asked the King. "Are there no places of amusement in my capital, no night restaurants? My Prefect of Police has closed all the night houses; but are there any the fewer open? However, I shall not need to enter the clubs. I shall find what I want in the streets, and on the benches."

Barely dressed, Christophe V skipped over Madame de la Poule, who was twisting in convulsions on the floor, dashed down the stairs, and ran across the garden. The dismayed Quatrefeuilles and Saint-Sylvain followed him afar off in silence.

CHAPTER X

WHETHER HAPPINESS CONSISTS IN NO LONGER BEING CONSCIOUS OF ONESELF

EACHING the main road, shaded by old elms, which bordered the Royal Park, he perceived a man, young, of wonderful beauty, who, leaning against a tree, was contemplating with an expression of delight the stars, which traced in the pure sky their sparkling and mysterious signs. His curly locks were shaken by the breeze; in his eyes there shone a reflection of the heavenly brilliance.

"I have found it!" thought the King.

He approached this handsome, smiling young man, who started slightly at the sight of him.

"I must apologize, sir," said the sovereign, "for disturbing your meditation. But the question which I am about to put to you has, for me, a vital interest. Do not refuse to reply to a man who is perhaps in a position to oblige you, and who will not be ungrateful. Sir, are you happy?"

"I am."

"Is there nothing lacking to your happiness?"

"Nothing. To be sure, it has not always been so. Like all other men, I have felt the evils of life; perhaps I have felt them more grievously than most. They befell me owing neither to my private condition nor to fortuitous circumstances, but to the essential basis, common to all men, and everything that breathes. I did know a great uneasiness; it has entirely disappeared. I enjoy perfect calm, and sweet cheerfulness: all within me is contentment, serenity, and a deep satisfaction: I am penetrated throughout by a subtle joy. You meet me, sir, at the most beautiful moment of my life, and since fortune has caused me to meet you, I will take you as witness to my happiness.

"At last I am free, exempt from all the fears and terrors by which men are assailed, from the ambitions which eat them up, and the crazy hopes which devour them. I am above Fate: I am escaping from man's two invincible enemies, Space and Time. I am able to defy Destiny. I possess absolute Happiness, and merge myself in the Divine. This happy condition is my own work: it is due to a resolution I have taken, so wise, good, beautiful, virtuous, and efficacious, that in grasping it one is deified.

"I swim in joy, I am magnificently intoxicated. With full consciousness, and in the sublime plenitude of its meaning, I pronounce this phrase of all frenzies, raptures, and enthusiasms: 'I no longer know myself!'"

He pulled out his watch and said:

"The hour is come. Good-bye."

"One word more, sir. You can save me. I——"

"One can only be saved by following my example. You must leave me here. Good-bye!"

And the unknown, with an heroic step and a youthful gait, darted into the wood bordering on the road. Christophe, regardless of his words, followed him. As he was entering the undergrowth he heard a report, stepped forward, brushed aside the branches, and saw the happy young man lying on the grass, his temple pierced by a bullet, still grasping a revolver in his right hand.

The King fainted at the sight. Quatrefeuilles and Saint-Sylvain, hastening up, helped him to recover his senses, and conveyed him to the Palace. Christophe made inquiries about the young man who had found such a desperate happiness under his eyes. He learned that he was the heir of a rich and noble family, as intelligent as he was handsome, and always a favourite of Fortune.

CHAPTER XI

SIGISMOND DUX

N the following day, Quatrefeuilles and Saint-Sylvain, still in search of the medicinal shirt, as they were walking down the Rue de la Constitution, met the Comtesse de Cécile, coming out of a music shop. They escorted her to her carriage.

"Monsieur de Quatrefeuilles," she said, "you were not visible yesterday at Professor Quilleboeuf's clinic; nor you either, Monsieur de Saint-Sylvain. You were wrong not to come; it was very interesting. Professor Quilleboeuf had invited all the fashionable world to his operation at five o'clock, a delightful ovariotomy. It was both crowded and select. There were flowers, smart dresses, and music; ices were served. The Professor exhibited wonderful grace and elegance. He had films taken for the cinematograph."

This description did not greatly surprise Quatrefeuilles. He knew that Professor Quilleboeuf operated to an accompaniment of luxury and pleasure: he would have asked him for his shirt if a few days previously he had not seen the famous surgeon inconsolable because he had not operated on the two greatest celebrities of the day, the German Emperor, who had just had a cyst removed by Professor Hilmacher, and the dwarf at the Folies-Bergères, who, having swallowed a hundred nails, objected to having her stomach opened, and treated herself with castor oil.

Saint-Sylvain stopping in front of the music shop, contemplated the bust of Sigismond Dux, and uttered a loud cry:

"That's the man we're looking for. There's the happy man!"

The bust, a very good likeness, represented a noble and regular set of features; one of those full, harmonious faces which have a look of a globe of the world. Although very bald, and already old, the great composer appeared no less charming than magnificent. His cranium was as round as the dome of a church, but a rather thick nose was planted beneath it with a loving and profane robustness; a close-clipped beard failed to conceal the fleshy lips, an erotic and a Bacchic mouth. It was the very likeness of the genius who composed the most pious oratorios and the most passionate and sensual opera-music.

"Why," continued Saint-Sylvain, "did we never

think of Sigismond Dux, who so thoroughly enjoys his stupendous glory, is clever enough to seize all its advantages, and just madcap enough to spare himself the constraint and the boredom of high position: the most spiritual and most sensual of geniuses, happy as a god, serene as a beast, combining in his countless love-affairs the most brutal cynicism with the most exquisite delicacy?"

"He has a rich and varied temperament," said Quatrefeuilles. "His shirt can do His Majesty nothing but good. Let us go and seek him out."

They were introduced into a vast, sonorous chamber like a café concert hall. An organ, raised on three steps, covered one section of the wall with its case of innumerable pipes. Wearing a doge's cap, and a dalmatic of brocade, Sigismond Dux was improvising melodies, and under his fingers were born sounds which troubled the soul, and melted the heart. On the three steps, covered with purple, a group of seated women, magnificent or charming, long, thin and surpentine, or plump, compact, and of a splendid massiveness, all equally beautified by desire and love, burning and swooning, writhed at his feet. The whole hall was filled with a quivering crowd of young American women, Jewish financiers, diplomatists, dancers, singers, Catholic, Anglican and Buddhist priests, black princes, piano-tuners, reporters, lyric poets, photographers, men dressed as women, and women dressed as men. They were pressed together, mingled and amalgamated, and formed a single adoring mass. Above them, climbing the columns, astride the candelabras, and hanging to the lustres, swayed young and agile devotees. This vast crowd was swimming in a sea of intoxication: it was what is called a private performance.

The organ ceased. A cloud of women surrounded the Master, who half emerged from time to time, like a brilliant star, to dive back into it immediately. He was gentle, coaxing, lascivious, and slippery. Amiable, no more of a coxcomb than need be, big as the world, and pretty as a cherub, as he smiled he showed through his grey beard teeth like a young child's, and uttered, to each in turn, facile and pretty phrases with which they were delighted, and which could not be remembered, so airy were they, so that their charm remained unabated, embellished with mystery. He was equally pleasant and friendly with the men, and seeing Saint-Sylvain, he embraced him three times, and said he loved him dearly; the King's secretary lost not a moment; he asked for a few moments' confidential conversation on behalf of the King, and, having explained briefly the important mission with which he was entrusted, he said:

"Master, give me your sh——"

He stopped, noticing that Sigismond Dux's features had suddenly become distorted.

In the street a barrel-organ had begun to grind out "The Jonquil Polka." And at the very first bars the great man had turned pale.

This "Jonquil Polka," the rage of the season, had been composed by a miserable, obscure violinist, Bouquin by name, employed in a dancing hall, and the master, crowned with forty years of love and glory, could not bear that some small portion of praise should be diverted to Bouquin: he regarded it as an insupportable insult. God himself is jealous, and afflicted by man's ingratitude. Sigismond Dux could not hear "The Jonquil Polka" without falling ill.

He abruptly deserted Saint-Sylvain, his crowd of adorers, his magnificent flock of swooning women, and rushed to his dressing-room, where he was violently sick.

"He is to be pitied," sighed Saint-Sylvain.

And, dragging Quatrefeuilles by his coat-tails, he crossed the unfortunate musician's threshold.

CHAPTER XII

WHETHER VICE IS A VIRTUE

OR fourteen months, from morn to eve, from nightfall to daylight, they scoured the city and the suburbs, observing, examining, interrogating in vain. The King, who was losing strength from day to day and who now had some idea of the difficulties of such a quest, gave orders to the Minister of the Interior to institute a special commission, charged, under the direction of Messieurs Quatrefeuilles, Chaudesaigues, Saint-Sylvain, and Froidefond, to proceed, with full powers, to a secret inquiry on the subject of the happy persons in the kingdom. The Prefect of Police, in compliance with the Minister's wishes, placed his most capable subordinates at the disposal of the Commission, and in a very short space of time the happy were sought out, in the capital, with all the zeal and devotion which in other countries is devoted to hunting down wrongdoers and anarchists. Should a citizen be reputed fortunate he was immediately denounced, spied upon and tracked down. Two of the Prefect's officials dragged their heavy iron-soled boots without remission before the windows of anyone suspected of being happy. Did a man of fashion take a box at the opera he was immediately placed under supervision. An eye was kept on any owner of a training-stable whose horse won a race. In all houses of appointment a clerk of the Prefecture, seated in the office, took a note of those entering. On the remark of the Prefect of Police that Virtue was the source of happiness benefactors, founders of charitable institutions, generous givers, deserted but faithful wives, citizens remarkable for acts of devotion, heroes and martyrs were all alike denounced, and submitted to the most minute investigation.

This supervision weighed upon the whole city, but its reason was an absolute mystery. To no one had Quatrefeuilles and Saint-Sylvain confided that they were looking for a lucky shirt, for fear, as has been already explained, that ambitious people, or avaricious individuals feigning to enjoy a perfect happiness, should impose on the King, as a happy article, some article of clothing impregnated with misery, care, and disappointments.

The extraordinary measures of the Police scattered uneasiness among the upper classes, and there was a certain ferment noted in the city. Several highly respected ladies found themselves compromised, and there were outbursts of scandal.

The Commission met every morning at the Royal Library, under the presidency of Monsieur de Quatrefeuilles, assisted by Messieurs Trou and Boncassis, on special duty. At every sitting it examined an average of fifteen hundred reports. After a session of four months it had not yet secured a happy man.

As the President, Quatrefeuilles, was bewailing the situation, Monsieur Boncassis exclaimed:

"Alas, it is vice that causes us to suffer, and all men have vices!"

"I have none," said Monsieur Chaudesaigues, "and the result is that I am in despair. Life without vice is nothing but weariness, despondency, and sadness. Vice is the only distraction that one can taste in this world: vice is the colour of life, the salt of the soul, and the light of the mind. What do I say? vice is original, man's only creative power; it is the attempt of a natural organization against nature itself, of the enthronement of human sovereignty over animal sovereignty, of human creation over animal creation, of a conscious world in the midst of the universal unconsciousness: vice is man's sole personal property, his real patrimony, his true virtue in the correct sense of the word, since virtue is the fact of being man (*virtus*, *vir*).

"I have tried to acquire some; I have been unable to do so; it requires genius, a natural gift—an assumed vice is not a vice."

"Well," asked Quatrefeuilles, "what do you call vice?"

"I call vice an habitual predisposition to what the majority regard as evil and abnormal: that is to say, individual morality, individual strength, individual virtue, beauty, power, and genius."

"That's all right," said the Counsellor Trou, "it's only a matter of understanding one another."

But Saint-Sylvain strongly combated the librarian's opinion.

"Don't talk of vices," he said, "since you have none. You don't know what they are. I have some; I have several, and I can assure you that I derive thence less pleasure than inconvenience. There is nothing more fatiguing than a vice. One worries, heats oneself, and exhausts oneself in satisfying it, and when it is satisfied one only experiences an immense disgust."

"You would not speak thus, sir," answered Chaudesaigues, "if you had fine vices, noble, proud, imperious, lofty, really virtuous vices. But you have nothing but mean, fearful, ridiculous little vices. You are not, sir, a great affronter of the gods."

At first Saint-Sylvain felt hurt by this remark, but the librarian explained that there was nothing offensive in it. Saint-Sylvain agreed with a good grace, and with calmness and resolution made the following reflexion :

" Alas, virtue, like vice, and vice, like virtue, consists in effort, constraint, conflict, trouble, toil, and exhaustion ! That is why we are all unhappy."

But the President, Quatrefeuilles, complained that his head would burst.

" Gentlemen," he said, " please do not let us argue. We are not here for that."

And he closed the meeting.

The result of this Commission on Happiness was the same as that of all Commissions, Parliamentary, and extra-Parliamentary, in all times and in all countries : it ended in nothing, and, having sat for five years, it was dissolved after producing no useful result.

The King got no better. Neurasthenia, like the Old Man of the Sea, assumed various terrible shapes to bring him low. He complained of feeling that all his organs had become erratic, and were moving incessantly inside his body into unaccustomed positions, his kidneys into his gullet, his heart into his calf, his intestines into his nose, his liver into his throat, and his brain into his stomach.

" You cannot imagine," he said, " how painful

these sensations are, and how they throw one's ideas into confusion."

"Sire, I can appreciate it all the better," said Quatrefeuilles, "because in my youth it often happened that my stomach rose into my brain, and you can imagine how that upset my ideas. My mathematical studies suffered much in consequence."

The worse Christophe's sufferings, the more eagerly did he demand the shirt which had been prescribed for him.

CHAPTER XIII

MONSIEUR LE CURÉ MITON

" AM coming back to the idea," said Saint-Sylvain to Quatrefeuilles, "that the failure of our search is caused by our faulty method. I certainly believe in virtue and I believe in happiness. They are inseparable. They are rare. They conceal themselves. We shall find them under humble roofs in the depth of the country. If you agree, we will, for choice, seek them in that rugged mountain country which is our Savoy, our Tyrol."

A fortnight later they had investigated sixty mountain villages without finding a single happy man. In these hamlets they found all the miseries that distressed the towns, accentuated by the uncouthness and ignorance of the people. Love and hunger, those two scourges of nature, struck the miserable inhabitants with even harder and more urgent blows. They saw greedy masters, jealous husbands, lying wives, maid-servants who poisoned their employers, men-servants who murdered them, incestuous fathers, and children who emptied the kneading-trough over their grandfather's head as he sat dozing by the fireside. These peasants had no pleasure save drunkenness; even their joys were brutal, and their games cruel. Their holidays would end with bloody hand-to-hand fights.

The further they observed them, Quatrefeuilles and Saint-Sylvain recognized that the morals of these men could not be either better or purer, that the niggard earth made them mean, that a hard life made them callous to others' troubles, as also to their own, and that if they were jealous, covetous, false, liars, and incessantly busy in cheating one another, it was the natural effect of their misery and indigence.

"How could I have ever imagined that happiness dwelt under a thatched roof?" Saint-Sylvain asked himself. "It is probably due to a classical education. Virgil, in his administrative poem, the *Georgics*, says that the country-folk would be happy did they recognize their good fortune. He thereby admits that they do not know it. As a matter of fact, he was writing by the order of Augustus, an excellent steward of the Empire, who feared that Rome would lack bread, and was seeking to repopulate the country districts. Virgil, like every one else, knew that the life of the peasantry is a laborious one. Hesiod draws a frightful picture of it."

"One thing is certain," said Quatrefeuilles, "and that is, that in all parts of the world the country boys and girls have only one desire, to get work in a town. On the sea coast the girls dream of employment in a sardine factory. In the coal districts, the country lads long for nothing so much as to go down a mine."

One man, in these mountains, displayed, amid care-worn brows and frowning faces, an ingenuous smile. He could neither work on the land nor drive the beasts; he was ignorant of all that other men knew. His words were wanting in sense, and all day long he sang a little song which he never finished. He was delighted with everything, and lived among the angels. His coat was composed of scraps of every colour fantastically sewn together. The children used to follow him and make fun of him, but as he had the reputation of a luck-bringer nobody harmed him, and the little he needed was given him. He was Hurtepoix, the simpleton. He fed at the cottage doors, with the dogs, and slept in barns.

Seeing that he was happy, and suspecting that it was not without some reason that the country-folk regarded him as a luck-bringer, after much reflexion Saint-Sylvain sought him out to secure his shirt. He found him lying prostrate, weeping bitterly in the church porch. Hurtepoix had just learned of the death of Jesus Christ, crucified for the salvation of mankind.

Going down to a village where the mayor was an innkeeper, the two King's officers asked him to drink with them, and inquired if, by chance, he knew of a happy man.

"Gentlemen," he answered, "go to the village on the other side of the valley, whose white houses you see hanging to the mountain-side, and call on the Curé Miton; he will be glad to see you, and you will meet a happy man, who deserves his happiness. You will get there in two hours."

The mayor offered to hire them horses, and after lunch they set off.

A young man, travelling the same road, and better mounted, caught them up at the first bend. He had an open countenance, and an air of cheerfulness and health. They entered into conversation with him.

Learning that they were about to call on the Curé Miton, he said:

"Please give him my kind regards. I am going farther up to Sizeraie, where I live, in the midst of beautiful pastures. I am in a hurry to get there."

He told them that he had married the best and most loving of wives, and that she had presented him with two children, a boy and a girl, as beautiful as day.

"I am on my way from the country town," he added in a cheerful tone, "and I am taking back some handsome dresses in the piece, with patterns and plates of the fashions, which show the effect of the costume. Alice—my wife—has no idea of the present I am bringing her. I shall give her the parcels all wrapped up, and I shall have the pleasure of watching her impatient fingers worrying to undo the knots. She will be very pleased: her delighted eyes, full of a cool light, will raise themselves to mine, and she will kiss me. Alice and I are happy. We have been married four years, and love each other more every day. We have the richest meadows in the country-side. Our servants are happy too; they are fine reapers and dancers. You must come and see us some Sunday, gentlemen; you will drink our white wine, and you will watch at their dancing the most graceful girls in the country, and the strongest lads, who pick up their partners and make them fly round like a feather. Our home is half an hour from here. You turn to the right by those two rocks which you see fifty yards ahead, and which are called the Chamois-feet: then you go over a wooden bridge thrown across a torrent, and through the pine-wood which protects us from the north wind. In less than half an hour I shall be home, and we shall all four be very happy."

"We must ask him for his shirt," said Quatrefeuilles in a low voice to Saint-Sylvain. "I expect it is as good as that of the Curé Miton."

"I expect so," said Saint-Sylvain.

At the moment they were thus speaking a rider came down through the Chamois-feet, and stopped, sad and silent, before the travellers.

Recognizing one of his farm hands, the young master said:

"What's the matter, Ulric?"

Ulric made no reply.

"Has some misfortune happened? Speak!"

"Sir, your wife was anxious to see you again, and came down to meet you. The wooden bridge broke, and she was drowned in the torrent with both children."

Leaving the young mountaineer mad with grief, they went on to Monsieur Miton, and were received at the presbytery, in a room that served the curé both as parlour and as library. There were here a thousand volumes on pine shelves, and against the whitewashed walls hung old engravings of landscapes after Claude Lorrain and Poussin. Everything pointed to a culture and a habit of mind not usually encountered in a village presbytery.

Monsieur Miton, a middle-aged man, had a kind, intelligent air.

To his two visitors, who pretended that they

were desirous of settling in the country, he praised the climate, and the fertile beauty of the valley. He offered them white bread, fruit, cheese, and milk. He then led them into his kitchen garden, which was delightfully fresh and tidy. On the wall which received the sun the espaliers extended their branches with geometrical precision. The distaff-shaped fruit-trees stood at equal distances from one another, very regular and well laden.

"You are never bored, Monsieur le curé?" asked Quatrefeuilles.

"The time appears short between my garden and my library," answered the priest. "Quiet and peaceful as it is, my life is none the less active and laborious. I celebrate the offices, I visit the poor and sick, and I confess my parishioners. The poor creatures have not many sins to relate; can I complain of that? But they take a long time telling them. I have to set aside a certain amount of time to prepare my sermons and catechisms; catechisms, in particular, give me a lot of trouble, although I have been doing them for twenty years. Talking to children is such a serious matter; they believe everything they are told. I have also my hours of amusement; I go for walks; they are always the same, and they are infinitely varied. A landscape changes with the seasons, the days, the hours, and the minutes; it is always different and always new. In bad weather I pass the long evenings pleasantly with old friends, the chemist, the schoolmaster, and the magistrate. We indulge in music. My servant, Morine, excels in cooking chestnuts: we feast on them. What tastes better than chestnuts, with a glass of white wine?"

"Sir," said Quatrefeuilles to the good priest, "we are on His Majesty's service. We have come to ask you to make a statement, which will be of the greatest consequence to the country, and to the whole world. It is a matter of the King's health, and perhaps of his life. For this reason, we beg of you to excuse our question, strange and indiscreet as it may appear, and to answer without any concealment or reservation whatever. Monsieur le curé, are you happy?"

Monsieur Miton took Quatrefeuilles' hand, pressed it, and said in a voice so low as to be hardly audible:

"My life is a torture. I live a perpetual lie. I do not believe."

Two tears rolled down from his eyes.

CHAPTER XIV AND LAST

A HAPPY MAN

HAVING travelled through the country for a year in vain, Quatrefeuilles and Saint-Sylvain returned to the Château of Fontblande, whither the King had gone to enjoy the coolness of the woods. They found him in a state of prostration which was alarming the Court.

The guests did not lodge at the Château de Fontblande, which was hardly more than a hunting-box. The secretary and the equerry had taken lodgings in the village, and every day they walked through the woods to visit their Sovereign. On the way they often met a little man who lived in a great hollow plane-tree in the forest. His name was Mousque, and he was far from handsome, with his pug face, prominent cheek-bones, and large nose with round nostrils. But his square teeth, which his red lips often uncovered in laughter, gave his wild face an appearance of brightness and cheeriness. How he had taken possession of the great hollow plane-tree no one knew; but he had made himself a very tidy room there, furnished with all that he required. Truth to tell, he needed little. He lived on the forest and the lake, and he lived very well. The irregularity of his condition was overlooked, because he made himself useful, and knew how to please people. When the ladies at the château drove in the forest, he would offer them, in baskets of osier plaited by himself, sections of honey, wild strawberries, or the tart, sweet fruit of the wild cherry. He was always ready to put his shoulder to the wheel of a cart foundered in the mire, and would help to fetch in the hay if the weather was threatening. He would do more than others without getting tired. His strength and activity were extraordinary. He could break a wolf's jaw-bone with his hands, run down a hare, and climb trees like a cat. To amuse the children he made reed flutes, little windmills, and Hieron's fountains.

Quatrefeuilles and Saint-Sylvain often heard it said in the village: "Happy as Mousque." This proverb impressed their minds, and one day, passing the hollow plane-tree, they saw Mousque playing with a young puppy, and apparently as happy as the dog. It occurred to them to ask whether he was happy.

Mousque was unable to answer, not having reflected on the subject of happiness. They explained generally and very simply what it meant. After thinking it over for a moment he answered that he possessed it.

At this reply, Saint-Sylvain called out impetuously:

"Mousque, we will get you everything that you can want, gold, a palace, new shoes, anything that you would like: but give us your shirt."

His kindly face expressed neither regret nor disappointment, which he was quite incapable of feeling, but a great surprise. He made a sign that he could not give what they asked of him. He had not a shirt.

THE END

THE GREATEST LIVING FRENCHMAN OF LETTERS

Anatole France has lately declared that Socialism, in some form, is inevitable throughout the world, and is "the one hope for Europe."

www.ingramcontent.com/pod-product-compliance
Lightning Source LLC
Chambersburg PA
CBHW030342310726
48979CB00001B/145

* 9 7 8 1 4 3 4 4 7 0 6 2 1 *